The
Secret Cross
of Lorraine

The Secret Cross of Lorraine

THEA BROW

drawings by Allen Say

Parnassus Press Oakland California
Houghton Mifflin Company Boston 1981

A *Parnassus Press* Book

Library of Congress Cataloging in Publication Data
Brow, Thea.
    The secret cross of Lorraine.
    SUMMARY: While visiting friends in France, Twyla
becomes involved with trying to find the elusive
owner of a lost Cross of Lorraine.
    [1. Mystery and detective stories. 2. France—
Fiction] I. Say, Allen. II. Title.
PZ7.B79986Se   [Fic]   80–27646
ISBN 0–395–30344–3

For my mother,
and for everyone who shared the Bar-le-Duc
experience, especially those who are no
longer with us.

CONTENTS

The
Secret Cross
of Lorraine

1

A Stranger in the Rain

Twyla Jones stretched her legs out under the dashboard of the small German car. Her mother sat behind the steering wheel, humming softly to herself as she concentrated on the road ahead. Her eight-year-old brother, Nicholas, was in the back seat. The scene in the car was familiar. It seemed to Twyla she had spent a part of every day of her life being driven by Mom somewhere. But how different this scene really was from all those other days. This time they were going somewhere — somewhere new and, she hoped, exciting.

Just one month ago they were in their home in California. Then her father received orders to report to Frankfurt, Germany, to work in the American Consulate there. They had packed up their belongings, put some of their furniture in storage, and flown away on the jumbo jet to Germany and a new home for two years. And today they were on their way to France for a two-week holiday before the school year began. How lovely to be going somewhere different.

Twyla stretched again and stifled a lazy yawn.

Her mother noticed the movement and said, "We will be crossing the border soon. That's the Rhine River on the right. We will cross at Strasbourg and can stop there for a snack."

"Good," said Twyla. "I'm famished."

"How does that sound to you, Nicholas?" Mrs. Jones asked.

Nicholas was sprawled out on the back seat, utilizing every inch of space in much the same way he monopolized the sofa at home. The lush green countryside of Germany had lost its appeal to him shortly after their lunch stop in Heidelberg.

"Can we have some more of those fat hot dogs we had for lunch?" he asked.

"Bratwurst?" his mother asked.

"Yeah. They were good."

"They were also German," said Twyla. "Strasbourg is in France and we'll be eating French food there."

"We may find bratwurst on the menu," said Mrs. Jones. "Strasbourg used to be in Germany. That part of France has changed hands between the French and Germans many times in the past."

"What language do they speak?" asked Nicholas, who had been concerned with the difficulty of making himself

2

understood ever since they had moved to Germany.

"French," his mother answered. "But many people will speak and understand German, too."

Twyla added, "The Europeans speak many more languages than we do, Nicky. Most of them study English in school, too."

Nicholas muttered something under his breath and twirled the wheels of the skateboard he held upside down on his lap.

Twyla turned to her mother and grinned. "Nicky's more interested in finding a place to skateboard than he is in learning something about the culture of France and Germany."

"I remember a little girl with long blond hair who was just as interested in skateboards not so many years ago," Mrs. Jones said.

It was true. Twyla had once been a tomboy. She had even won the sixth-grade championship on the skateboard, forever alienating the sixth-grade boys she had so wanted to impress. Her father told her girls with spunk had to expect that.

Then she had changed her image. When they moved to California she enrolled in a ballet class and got a new wardrobe. She would never forget her first day of school in San Diego. She was dressed in a new skirt and blouse and all the other girls wore blue jeans. She had her hair cut shoulder length and the California girls wore theirs halfway down their backs. She had an Eastern pallor and they had deep tans. They were surfers — ocean surfers.

To make matters worse, most of her new friends were

tall and willowy. Twyla had stopped growing when her height reached five feet two inches. She felt like a cocker spaniel in the company of Great Danes.

Her father had assured her that he preferred short women. It was nice of him to say that, but it didn't make her feel any better when all the "Great Danes" were surfing with the boys and she was left on the beach with her mystery books.

So Twyla did what she always did when her family moved to a new place. She learned to do the things that her new friends did. She was becoming a fairly good surfer just when her father got word of his new assignment in Germany. It was bound to happen. It always did.

Twyla sighed, remembering her past frustrations. Her mind drifted to the present and she said, "Nicky is going to have fun trying to skateboard on cobblestones."

"They have parking lots in Europe," said Nicholas.

"In Frankfurt, maybe," said Twyla. "But at the Lamberts' bunker? I think not."

Nicholas was silent a moment, then asked, "What exactly is a bunker, Mom?"

"A bunker is a fortification," his mother answered, switching on the windshield wipers to clear off the few drops of rain that had appeared suddenly on the glass. "Oh, dear. Looks like France is welcoming us with a storm."

Twyla looked across the river to the west, where tall banks of black clouds had been building on the horizon all afternoon. She knew her mother didn't like to drive in the rain, especially over unfamiliar roads. But Twyla loved to ride in the rain. It made the inside of the car seem more cozy.

"You mean like the Roman fort we saw near Frankfurt last week?" Nicholas asked.

"A little like that," said Mrs. Jones. "But the Lamberts' bunker is newer. The Roman fort is two thousand years old. The bunkers of the Maginot Line were built in 1927, between World War I and World War II, to prevent the Germans from invading France."

"Did they?"

"Unfortunately not," his mother said. "But I'll have to continue this explanation later, Nick. We're getting close to the border crossing. Twyla, get out the maps and guide me through this maze, will you?"

Twyla was the navigator, a job her mother usually performed on family trips. But since business had kept her father in Frankfurt, unable to accompany them on this visit to France, Twyla had been promoted to her mother's old position. For the next ten minutes she studied the maps and road signs and directed her mother through the turns that led them to the German customs station at the border.

The rain was coming down harder, making it more difficult to see the road ahead. They inched across a bridge and through the French inspection station. A French border guard in uniform asked to see their passports, then waved them through without even asking to see their luggage.

"How do they know we're not smugglers or something?" Nicholas asked, a disappointed look on his face.

5

"We could be carrying anything in our trunk, for all they know."

"It's your honest face," said Twyla.

Nicholas made a funny face at her and she laughed. Half the time she found her young brother amusing. Half the time she found him annoying. The annoying times usually came when they both were tired and nerves were jangled. She hoped that wouldn't happen today. They were bound to be tired by the time they reached their destination this evening, and Mother had warned that she expected them to use their best manners during their visit with Madame Lambert and her son, Bernard.

Mrs. Jones and Cécile Lambert had been friends in college twenty years before. Madame Lambert was an exchange student from France for a year and had roomed with Twyla's mother. When she returned to France, she and Mrs. Jones had kept the friendship alive through letters. Both women had married and raised families. Madame Lambert's husband had died in an accident two years ago, leaving her with a seriously ill son. But Bernard was now recuperating satisfactorily, according to her last Christmas letter.

Twyla loved to meet new people and see new places. She was curious about the Lamberts' summer home in an old bunker, but she knew it was located in an isolated area in the hills rising above the Rhine River valley and she imagined there wouldn't be a lot to do once the initial excitement wore off — especially since the only person close to her age was an invalid, probably not up to hiking or sightseeing. She had packed a dozen books

6

in her suitcase to read in case boredom set in.

Nicholas had also come prepared to entertain himself. He had his beloved skateboard with him, of course. And he had a box that held the precious pieces of his latest project — a model of the dirigible *Hindenburg*, which he was building. That should keep him occupied, Twyla hoped. Nicholas could be a very trying boy when bored.

The border crossing was accomplished easily and Twyla directed her mother to the correct turnoff to take them away from the center of Strasbourg toward the south. They had been in France about twenty minutes when they spotted a pleasant-looking café on the roadside. Mrs. Jones parked in the lot outside and they went in for the promised snack.

"Perhaps the rain will have passed over us by the time we've had our supper," Mrs. Jones said.

They ordered omelets, with a side order of bratwurst for Nicholas. Their food was served with the most delicious bread Twyla had ever tasted.

Her mother said, "Breads are my favorite treats in France. Wait until you've tasted croissants. My mouth waters thinking about them."

"I like the hot dogs best," said Nicholas.

"You would," said Twyla. She read the menu and said, "I don't see croissants listed here."

"You may not find them on the menu but they are served everywhere in the morning as part of the *petit déjeuner*, or breakfast," her mother answered.

Their table was next to the windows looking out over

the road. As they ate they watched the rain, which, unfortunately, did not pass as Mrs. Jones had hoped.

It was almost dark when they left the café, and the rain was heavier. Low clouds shrouded the hills to the west. Twyla shivered and pulled her sweater around her shoulders as she settled in the front seat next to her mother.

They followed the main road south for about ten kilometers, then turned west at a crossroads marked "St. Germain." This secondary road was less heavily traveled and they saw fewer and fewer houses as they climbed up into the hill country. The rain pounded on the windshield and Mrs. Jones was forced to slow down. Twyla couldn't see more than twenty feet ahead of the car.

They drove for a half-hour on an ever narrowing and rising road until finally Mrs. Jones stopped the car. They hadn't seen another automobile or sign of life for several kilometers. The sound of the rain on the roof was deafening. Mrs. Jones had to shout to be heard.

"We should have been there by now. You don't suppose we took a wrong turn somewhere?"

Twyla peered out the side window. A terraced hillside rose abruptly from the road.

"I've been watching very carefully, Mother. I haven't seen a sign since the turnoff marked 'St. Germain.' Madame Lambert's letter said we would find their sign along this road — the road to St. Germain."

"I know, dear, but in this rain . . ." Mrs. Jones shook her head as she looked out the window. "Nothing but vineyards. We could have got off the road somewhere and if we're on vineyard property, on a private road, there would be no signs."

"Maybe we can find a village and call Madame Lambert for directions," Twyla suggested.

Her mother shook her head. "There's no phone at the bunker. That's why Cécile gave me such detailed directions in her letter."

Nicholas was sound asleep in the back seat. Twyla and her mother exchanged worried looks. Then her mother started up the engine again and continued driving slowly along the road. They both looked hard, hoping to see some sign of life. They concentrated so completely on the little patch of road visible in the headlights that neither was prepared for what happened next.

The figure of a man on a bicycle loomed up from out of the darkness. Mrs. Jones slammed on the brakes and the car fishtailed to the right as it slid off the road. The motor died but the lights still stabbed the rainy darkness. They could see nothing but the rain and a stretch of empty road.

"Where's the man on the bicycle?" Mrs. Jones said. "Oh, dear! You don't suppose we hit him?"

Twyla and her mother jumped out of the car from opposite sides and met in the glow of the headlights. There was no sign of the man or the bicycle.

"Where could he have gone?" Twyla asked.

Her mother shrugged. Just then they heard a very angry voice muttering words in French. That was followed by the scraping noise of something being dragged

9

over the pavement. They walked to the rear of the car in time to see the man picking himself up off the ground. One of his legs was stuck through the center bar of his bicycle and he swore to himself as he extricated the leg from the twisted metal.

Mrs. Jones rushed to his side to help. Twyla stood back, staring at his angry face, a little frightened by what she saw.

Mrs. Jones spoke to him in halting French. "Are you hurt? May I help?"

He pushed her back with a rough gesture and Twyla rushed to her mother's side. The man glared at them both, then looked down at his wrecked bicycle. He threw his arms into the air in a gesture of hopelessness.

Nicholas woke up and called to them from the car. "What happened?"

"A small accident, Nicky," his mother answered. "It's all right now." She turned to the man and asked, again in French, "Are you hurt, *monsieur?*"

The man shook his head and replied in English, "No. I am not hurt. But you have ruined my bike. *Sacrebleu!*"

"I am sorry. But you appeared so unexpectedly, from nowhere it seemed. Here, let me help you. We can put your bicycle on the car and drive you home."

The man hesitated and for a moment Twyla thought he would decline. Indeed, she hoped he would decline. He frightened her. His eyes glared and his face had a scraggly white beard. He was covered from head to foot by a dark-green poncho made of a waterproof material, but she could see through the slits at the sides of the garment that the clothes underneath were soiled and badly worn. He reminded her of the men she had seen hanging around the seedy part of her home town — the poor, unfortunate men who drink cheap wine and lounge along skid row.

Her mother seemed to have none of this fear. She put her arm on the man's shoulder and said, "Come. I will help you."

Mrs. Jones helped him drag the bike to the car. The man got into the back seat next to a wide-eyed Nicholas. He closed the door and Mrs. Jones handed him the bike, which he held to the side of the car through the open window.

"I think we can manage like this if your arm doesn't get too tired. I'm sorry we don't have any rope to tie it on for you."

The man grunted an unintelligible answer. Mrs. Jones and Twyla got into the car. Twyla shivered, as much from fear as from the soaking she had received in the rain.

"Where do you live?" Mrs. Jones asked the man.

"Just up the road. Not far. Two kilometers maybe. I will show you," the man answered.

He spoke English well, but as though he hadn't used it for a long time. Twyla couldn't discern any trace of accent in his speech, but she knew he must be French, since he had spoken that language at first, before he had realized they were American.

Mrs. Jones started the engine and, with some difficulty, got the car back onto the road.

"Perhaps you can help us," she said to the man. "We are looking for the Lamberts' home. It should be around here somewhere but we haven't seen any road signs for quite a while."

Twyla stole a look at the man in the back seat. He looked back at her with a curious glint in his eyes, not at all friendly. Was it fear she saw there?

"Stop here," he said abruptly. "I will get out here."

Twyla looked outside and could see no sign of a road or house. Nothing but trees on both sides of the road.

Mrs. Jones stopped the car. "Are you sure?"

"Here," the man repeated. "The people you seek are farther down this road. Not far."

Mrs. Jones pulled some money from her purse and handed it to the man. "Please take this to help pay for the repair of your bicycle."

He glared at her, pushed her hand aside, and opened the door. He got out, slammed the door, and walked away from them, carrying his battered bike under one arm. He didn't say good-by or thank you or anything. He didn't even look back.

"A very curious man," said Mrs. Jones.

Nicholas closed the window and said, "Boy, what a creep!"

"No, Nicholas. Just an old man, slightly confused and angry. I do hope he wasn't hurt."

Twyla didn't share her mother's opinion of the stranger, but she held her tongue. Her mother always said if you can't say something nice about someone, don't say anything at all. She couldn't think of one nice thing to say about this strange person except, "I'm glad he's gone."

Mrs. Jones patted her hand. "Me too," she said, and smiled. "Now let's see if the directions he gave us to the Lamberts' house were correct."

2

A Home in the Bunker

Around the next bend, less than a kilometer from where the stranger had left the car, they came to a side road. A sign bore the single and most welcome name *Lambert*. Mrs. Jones turned the car onto the one-lane dirt road and drove slowly up the winding way. The going was steep and rough.

Another sign directed them to turn off into an even smaller lane, at the end of which was a parking place built right into the side of the hill. Mrs. Jones parked next to a yellow car with French license plates. Their headlights illuminated the area and they saw a stairway built into the hill with another sign beside it, attached to an old-fashioned lightpost. They had no sooner stopped than the light on the post was turned on and a woman appeared on the stairs.

She was pretty and small, with short curly hair framing a pleasant smiling face. Twyla watched as her mother jumped out of the car and ran to embrace her old friend. The women held each other at arms length; Madame Lambert kissed Mrs. Jones on both cheeks, in the French manner, then stood back, and the two women looked at each other once again. All the time both squealed excitedly in French and English. They looked like two schoolgirls meeting after a long holiday apart.

Madame Lambert turned her attention next to Twyla and Nicholas. Both received kisses and hugs, and then she said, in English, "We must get out of this rain. Come. I will help you with your bags. You must get out of these wet things immediately before you catch cold."

As she led them up the steep stairway Twyla's eyes searched for some sign of a house or a fort, but she could see only the trees on the left and the hillside on the right, which rose steeply above the parked cars.

At the top of the stairs was a flat grassy area and a front door built right into the side of the hill. The door was open and a glow from inside welcomed them and lighted the grassy yard. A large yellow dog stood in the doorway, his tail wagging a quiet greeting. Nicholas dropped to his knees to pet him and received a wet kiss in return.

Farther back in the yard Twyla could see cement walls jutting from the cliff. There were two large French doors leading to a patio area, where lounge chairs and a metal table stood dripping in the rain.

"We live like moles," Madame Lambert said, laughing. "Partly underground. Leave your bags here in the hall. We will take them down to your rooms presently. But for now come to the fire."

Twyla was prepared for anything but the luxury she found in this unusual home. There were the French doors leading out to the side yard and, on another wall, a huge window overlooking the valley. Next to that was a sliding glass door that led out to a wooden deck. Half of the room was furnished like a family room, with soft leather chairs and low coffee tables. A large round dining table stood near the deck area, and beyond was a kitchen bar.

The kitchen made up the rest of the room. It seemed to be built around a free-standing fireplace, where Madame Lambert had a fire burning. The metal chimney rose straight up and disappeared into the cement ceiling above. Copper pots and pans decorated the walls and hung from hooks over a butcher block near the sink counter.

The whole living area had been painted in bright colors, mostly yellows and greens, and it was hard to imagine it had ever been a wartime bunker used by soldiers and furnished with cannons.

"What a lovely room," Mrs. Jones said as Madame Lambert helped them out of their wet garments.

"Thank you. My husband designed it, as he did the whole project, before he died. He was an architect, you know. It is a pity he did not live to see the results of his plans. The windows and deck are new. Some of the concrete walls had to be removed, and the plumbing and wiring are all new. But not necessarily good," she added, laughing. "I have been having much trouble with our power system. We keep candles handy at all times. The rest of the bunker is the original — your rooms and, of course, the tower."

Twyla thought Nicholas's eyes would pop out of his head as he said, "Wow! Where's the tower?"

Madame Lambert pointed to a spiral staircase beyond the kitchen area. "Up those stairs. Would you like to see it?"

She led them to the stairs and said, "Bernard's room is up here. He has been resting most of the day."

"I hope our being here won't upset him, Cécile," said Twyla's mother.

"On the contrary," Madame Lambert said. "It is just what he needs. He had a very bad fever just after his father died and he missed a year of school. But he has been well for a long time now. He needs the stimulation of young people around him."

They followed her up the spiral stairs to the first level of the tower. Twyla could see a slit of light shining at the bottom of the door. The light went out when Madame Lambert knocked. Then she heard a soft masculine voice answer, *"Entrez."*

Madame Lambert opened the door and said, "Our guests are here, Bernard. Perhaps you can join us downstairs?"

"Oui, Maman," said Bernard.

Madame Lambert closed the door and turned to the others. "I think he was sleeping. Let's give him time to get dressed. In the meantime come see the den. I am sleeping there while you are visiting."

They again climbed the stairs, this time to the highest level of the tower. At the top was a room with windows all around. Each window had a tiny garden growing on the sill — marigolds and daisies and violets and some white flowers Twyla had never seen before. There was a sofa bed and a desk. Under each window was a bookcase.

"Lovely," said Mrs. Jones.

Twyla went to one of the windows and looked out. Rain beat at the glass and it was very dark outside, but fingers of light shining from the downstairs rooms penetrated the wet night.

"It's like being in the middle of clouds," she said.

"On a clear day the view is spectacular," said Madame Lambert. "The soldiers who were stationed here could see the entire approach from the Rhine down our valley. Of course they never had a chance to use their advantage when the war started. Pity. It was such a good idea."

"Why didn't they?" asked Nicholas.

"Because when the Germans invaded in 1940 they didn't take the expected route across the Rhine and into France. Instead, they first invaded Belgium in the north and marched south across an almost undefended border. All the guns here in the Maginot Line were pointed in the wrong direction," Madame Lambert explained.

As she led them back down the stairs she asked, "Are you very hungry after your long drive?"

"We did have a light supper near Strasbourg," Mrs. Jones answered.

"That will never last you until breakfast. I will help carry the bags to your rooms and after you have had a chance to settle in then we will have something to eat. *Bien?*"

"*C'est bien,*" Mrs. Jones answered, and then she and her old friend spoke in French together as they struggled with the bags down the steep stairs that led to the bedrooms. Twyla had never heard her mother converse in French before and she felt a little left out. She could understand only a small part of what was said. One whole year in Madame Kaminsky's French class hadn't prepared her very well, she thought. French speakers never seemed to use the words and phrases she had learned in class.

Soon Twyla forgot the conversation. She was too busy discovering another part of the bunker. At the bottom of the stairs a long, dark hallway stretched out before them and ended at a heavy steel door. On their left were three smaller doors to the bedrooms. Madame Lambert took them past the first two doors to the third, and stopped.

"This is your room, Twyla," she said and opened the door to reveal a small room decorated in red, white, and blue. The far wall bulged out in a semicircle and had a long curved window at eye level.

"It was once a gun emplacement," Madame Lambert explained. "A pillbox I think you call it in English. All of the rooms down here are the same. We put up the inner walls to make separate bedrooms and had windows made to fit the openings. Before, they had only steel blinders to close up the slits against the weather. It is a cozy room and I hope you will be comfortable here. You will find the view quite enchanting tomorrow. And if you feel the need to warm the air, there is an electric heater here near the dresser. It is quite safe to use," she added, for Mrs. Jones's benefit. "The elements are enclosed, so there is no danger of burning yourself on it."

Madame Lambert opened the top drawer of the dresser. "Here is your flashlight. For use when the generator gives out. You each have one."

Twyla put her suitcase at the foot of the bed and admired the blue-and-white fleur-de-lis-patterned spread, which matched the ruffled curtain. The floor was covered with a white shaggy rug that she longed to sink her bare toes into. Mother would never have allowed a white rug at home. Twyla hoped Nicholas's room was furnished with a more practical floor covering.

It was. Nicky's room had a dark-brown rug and the color scheme was in browns and oranges, with a touch of yellow for accent. Twyla found this room very pleasing, too.

Mrs. Jones's room was just like her children's but the colors were in the green spectrum, with touches of yellow and white in the patterned bedspread.

Madame Lambert showed them where they could hang their clothes and where the bathroom was. Then she said, "There, you have your places. Now you must

LAMBERT'S BUNKER: CUTAWAY VIEW FROM WEST

BRICKED UP WALL

TUNNEL TO RUINED TOWER

STEEL DOOR

MUSHROOM RM.

KITCHEN

DINING

LIVING

BEDROOMS

CARPORT

freshen up and become acquainted with your new home, and I will get the supper on the table. *Bien?*"

Nicholas poked his head out of his room and pointed to the end of the hall. "What's behind that big door?" he asked.

"It leads to more pillboxes and tunnels. We haven't been through them all yet. Some are in very poor condition and I am afraid might be unsafe. The steel door keeps out the cold and the little animals that might be down there," Madame Lambert said.

"What kind of animals?" Nicky asked, and Twyla could almost hear the wheels in his head turning.

His mother interrupted. "I don't think I care to know the answer to that. I'm glad you have the solid door between us and them, anyway."

Twyla agreed, secretly, with her mother. But she shared some of her brother's curiosity, too.

Madame Lambert left them and Twyla went to her room to get the feel of it. She plopped down on the bed and kicked off her shoes. Then she stood up and walked around the room, letting her feet enjoy the lush pile of the fluffy white rug.

3

Enter Bernard

They had just settled down at the supper table when Bernard entered. Twyla could see his approach from where she sat. He was tall, very thin, and walked with a loose, disjointed gait. He had a long, sensitive face, very dark eyes, and a mouth set in a grim straight line, as though he were forcing himself to look serious.

Madame Lambert's smile widened when she saw him. "Here's Bernard," she announced. Then she made the introductions around the table.

Bernard acknowledged the introductions properly but with no sign of good humor. His mother, as though making up for his lack of warmth, smiled broadly enough for both of them. Twyla did not think he looked well, but she noted that he could be quite handsome if only he would smile.

Bernard offered little to the pleasant small talk at the table and seemed to concentrate on his food and on avoiding eye contact with Twyla and Nicholas. He did raise his eyes to meet hers once, when she related the incident on the road.

Twyla described how they thought they were lost, and how the man on the bicycle appeared like a ghost out of the blackness and headed straight for them, forcing Mrs. Jones to brake hard.

"Mother and I expected to find him dead on the road when we got out of the car. But he stood up right away and seemed unhurt."

"Thank goodness," said Twyla's mother.

Madame Lambert looked shocked. "But who was this stranger out in such a storm? Did he tell you his name?"

"No," Mrs. Jones answered. "But he must be a neighbor of yours. He asked to be let out just a short distance from here. And he knows where you live. He directed us to your road."

Madame Lambert shook her head. "But we have no neighbors. We are alone here on this hill. The closest farmhouse is several kilometers away, isn't that right, Bernard?"

Bernard didn't look up from the apple he was paring. "A vagabond, perhaps. Or a man running from the law."

Twyla shivered. "And we invited him into our car!"

Bernard shrugged. "He was no doubt harmless and by now is far away from here."

Nicholas had finished his meal and sat back in his chair swinging his energetic legs. It was obvious he was anxious to be up and moving about. His busy hands fidgeted with the ornament he wore on a string around his neck.

Bernard looked at him and changed the subject. "I see you wear the Cross of Lorraine," he said.

"Is that what it is?" Nicholas asked.

Twyla had never seen the cross before and asked, "Where did you get it, Nicky?"

"I found it in the car when we took the suitcases out."

"But where did it come from?"

Nicholas shrugged. Bernard asked to see it and Nicholas took it off and handed it to the older boy, who turned it over and inspected it carefully.

"Very fine work," Bernard said. "Quite old."

Nicholas looked pleased. "Is it worth a lot of money?"

"I don't know. There is an inscription, did you know? It says, 'T.L. for valor' and it is dated June 1942."

"No kidding?" said Nicholas. He took back the cross and looked at it with added appreciation.

"Do you suppose the old man dropped it in the car?" Twyla asked.

"If so," said her mother, "we surely must try to find him again so we can return it."

Nicholas's smile vanished. "You mean I can't keep it?"

"I'm afraid not. Not if we can find who owns it." Mrs. Jones looked at her son's face. "But I can see no harm in your wearing it until we do."

"And if he is a vagabond, as Bernard suggests, we may never find him again," said Madame Lambert.

Twyla thought of the old man, remembering his shabby clothes. It disturbed her to think that he may have lost the one thing of value he possessed. And his bicycle had been ruined, too, or at least very badly damaged.

"Do you know the significance of the Cross of Lorraine?" Bernard asked. Then he spoke without giving them a chance to say yes or no. "It was the symbol of the French Underground during World War II. The Free French had a large resistance operation during the Nazi occupation of France. They bombed German positions and stole ammunition. And they operated radio networks for secret communications with England and the other Allies."

"Gosh," said Nicholas. He held the cross in one hand as though it had become a living thing. "Do you think the old man was a secret agent?"

For the first time that evening Bernard cracked a smile, albeit a very small one. "Perhaps. The inscription says 'for valor' and the date was during the occupation. I have many books on World War II in my room. If you would like, I'll show you some very interesting pictures in them. I even have pictures of the Maginot Line bunkers as they looked before the war."

Bernard looked at Twyla and added, "You may come, too, if you like. Though I am told American girls are not much interested in such things."

Twyla bristled. "I have studied some history," she

26

answered. At this moment she wished it had been more.

"Have you read Churchill's books on the subject?" Bernard asked.

"Well, no . . ." she started. She wasn't about to admit that her free reading was made up mainly of mystery stories.

"It doesn't matter," said Bernard, standing and turning. "Come along. You may enjoy it."

His tone of voice implied that he didn't think she would. Twyla followed Bernard and Nicky upstairs. Her cheeks felt hot and she knew she was blushing. She always blushed when she was angry. How dare he assume that, because she was a girl, she would not be interested in serious subjects?

Madame Lambert called after them, "Come join us by the fire when you are through."

Bernard's room was a carbon copy of the other tower room except for one blank wall, which concealed the stairway. There were windows all around and bookcases beneath them. Bernard's bed also doubled as a sofa, and next to it was a large table, desk high, which was littered with open books and papers. It seemed to Twyla that Bernard had been studying, not sleeping, as his mother had suggested.

Two of the windows were covered by roll-down shades. These were different from ordinary shades. They had maps drawn on them, like the maps in school that hang above the blackboard and can be pulled down for viewing and then, when not needed, rolled back up out of the way. The maps that were now pulled down were of the Western Hemisphere. There was one of the United States and one of South America. When they entered the room Bernard crossed to the maps and rolled them up, then pulled down another one, covering a third window.

"Would you like to see where you are?" he asked. He pointed to a zigzag line on the map stretching from Longwy, in northeastern France, to the Rhine River and south to the Swiss border. "This is the Maginot Line," he said. "All along this line are bunkers similar to the one we are in now. We are located right here."

His finger jabbed at a point just west and a little south of Strasbourg. Nicholas was attentive, clearly worshiping the older boy who spoke with such a professorial air. Twyla thought Bernard was showing off a little too much to suit her. She knew where they were. She had been reading the map for her mother all day.

She busied herself at a bookcase, studying the French titles. Her father always said, "Show me a man's library and I'll tell you what kind of person he is." All she could tell from these books was that Bernard had an interest in history and armaments. The books seemed very serious reading to Twyla. Not a title on the shelves appealed to her. She noticed one dust jacket more colorful than the others, with "Jeanne d'Arc" on it, and pulled it from the shelf. That was a title she at least recognized, and the book appeared to have more to offer than the others. She sat down in a chair near the desk and began riffling through the pages as Bernard's voice droned on.

"Here is a diagram you may like, Nicholas," Bernard continued. "It's a cutaway of a bunker, showing the tunnels and the various levels. This particular bunker has six levels built down into the ground."

"Golly!" said Nicholas.

"You can see they were well equipped. They had air conditioning, large dining halls, showers, reading rooms, and cinemas. All underground."

Twyla peeked at the diagram.

"But if everyone lived underground, how could they hear the enemy?" Nicholas asked.

"There were always lookouts stationed in the towers, much like the tower you are in now. The lookouts kept watch around the clock."

"Does your bunker go down in the ground as deep as this one in the diagram?" Nicholas asked.

"I don't know yet," Bernard answered. "There is a level below your bedrooms that is open and cleared out. My mother wants to grow mushrooms down there and we have explored it a bit. But many years ago the passages were sealed off or collapsed and Mother won't let me poke around too much for fear it is unsafe. Someday we will hire an engineer to test the walls for us."

"Golly!" Nicholas said again.

Twyla buried her head in the Joan of Arc book but her thoughts were on the caverns Bernard had described. The prospect of that open space below her bedroom fascinated her. Secret tunnels and rooms and who knew what, might be found underground! It was too much to be dismissed as casually as Bernard seemed to dismiss it.

If she lived in the bunker she would spend all her time exploring.

"How did you get this old place, anyway?" Nicholas asked.

"In 1975 the government put some bunkers up for sale," Bernard answered. "People began buying them for use as tourist sites, museums, and even summer homes, as my father did. My father bought ours for me. He wanted me to own a piece of history for the future."

Twyla thought she heard his voice crack as he spoke the last words. But his face betrayed none of the emotion he might be feeling at the moment. He turned his back on Nicholas and walked past Twyla on his way to the door.

Seeing the book on her lap, he said, "You like Joan of Arc? She lived in this part of France. Not far from here. Her symbol, too, was the Cross of Lorraine."

He walked out the door and Twyla and Nicholas scrambled to follow. They joined their mothers by the fire, where they were offered hot chocolate and cookies.

Bernard excused himself early and went up to his room. After he had gone, Nicholas read a book on airships that Bernard had lent him.

Twyla lay on her stomach on the floor, watching the fire dance and spit, and listened to the storm outside. She was engrossed by the reminiscences of her mother and Madame Lambert. They talked about their days together at the university and their lives since. Madame Lambert spoke briefly of her husband's death in an automobile accident two years before, and of the effect it had on her and especially on Bernard.

"It was so sudden," she said. "Bernard was away at school when it happened. When he came home he would sit in a room as though he were waiting for his father to walk in at any moment. I don't think he ever accepted the fact that his father was no longer living."

Bernard had fallen ill a short time later. The doctors said his fever was probably brought on by the severe shock of losing his father. He recovered but had lost a year of school and had grown very introspective. Madame Lambert was anxious to have him go out more with young people now that he was better, but he seemed to prefer the company of his books.

"Sociability," said Madame Lambert, "is a habit that must be cultivated when one has been cut off for so long a time. What he needs now is more people around him."

Twyla had her own ideas of what Bernard needed, starting with some brisk outdoor activity in the sunshine and maybe a black eye from a neighborhood ruffian to knock him off his high horse. She squirmed uncomfortably at the last thought. It wasn't that she wished him harm. If only he weren't so . . . so well informed, she thought.

Later, when they had retired to their rooms, Twyla lay in bed in the cozy little pillbox room trying to fall asleep. It had been a stimulating day, with the long drive from Germany and the encounter on the rain-slick road with the strange old man. And meeting new people always excited her, too. Then, of course, there was this bunker to think about.

She tried to block all those thoughts from her mind and concentrate on the soft bed and her exhaustion. Still, she could not forget that behind the steel door in the hallway outside her room were tunnels and basement caverns and who knew what?

She dozed off only to awaken some time later realizing that something was different about her surroundings. She was very drowsy and it took several moments for her to notice that the rain and wind outside had stopped. It was lighter than it had been before. The moon was shining into her room, casting a slash of yellow light against the wall next to her bed.

She snuggled down farther under the fluffy comforter, closed her eyes, and began to drop off to sleep when she heard something that jolted her awake again. It was a faint clink, clink that she heard. It stopped as suddenly as it had begun. At first she thought her ears were playing tricks on her. Then it started again, this time sounding like a hammer on metal, but very faint, as though it were a long way off — as though there were a blacksmith at work deep in the bowels of this hill . . .

Twyla fell asleep and dreamed all night of inner-earth trolls and witches' caldrons and nameless creatures scratching on a big steel door.

4

The Man Who Wasn't
There in St. Germain

Sunlight had replaced the moonlight in
Twyla's room when she woke up. She jumped out of bed
and ran to the window to see what was outside. Below
her and as far as her eyes could see were tree-clad hills
leading down to the valley. In the distance was flat country and, she knew, the Rhine River, though it was not
visible from her window. The sky was blue and clear of
all clouds. It was the kind of day that begged to be enjoyed out of doors.

Twyla dressed and ran to her mother's room. The
door was open and a young woman was inside making
the bed.

"*Bonjour,*" the girl said in a lyrical voice. Her smile
was warm and friendly.

33

"*Bonjour,*" Twyla answered. "I am looking for my mother."

The girl pointed to the ceiling and said, "She is with Madame Lambert above. You have slept very long."

Twyla looked at her wrist watch. It was just a little past eight. Not late at all. In fact it seemed early to Twyla. She said good-by to the girl, who obviously had been awake and busy since dawn, and hurried upstairs.

She found her mother and Madame Lambert finishing up their breakfast coffee at the dining table. Gitano, the large yellow dog she had met briefly the night before, lazed on the deck outside. She could see a larger panorama of the valley behind him.

"*Bonjour, Maman. Bonjour, Madame Lambert,*" she said taking a place at the table.

"You are feeling at home, then?" Madame Lambert asked her in French.

Twyla answered, also in French, that she felt very French this morning. Then, lapsing into English, she added, "The girl downstairs just said '*bonjour*' to me and it sounded so cheery that I decided to use the greeting myself."

"And it is a good day," her mother added.

"Marie is a pleasant girl," Madame Lambert said. "She comes every morning from the village to help me. And she brings with her, besides her own good humor, my breakfast."

"Try some of these, Twyla," Mrs. Jones said, pushing a plate of croissants toward her daughter.

Twyla picked up a golden-brown roll shaped like a

crescent, broke it in half so that the tender buttery inside was exposed, and took a bite. Now she knew what her mother had meant. The flaky, crunchy outside melted at the touch of her tongue and the flavor was exquisite. The croissant needed no garnish of butter or jelly, though both were on the table.

Also on the table were a yellow basket of boiled eggs, a basket of crusty French bread, a pitcher of orange juice, and a pot of café au lait.

Twyla helped herself and asked, "Is Nicky still sleeping?"

"No. He has been up for an hour. He ate and went off somewhere," Mrs. Jones answered.

"With Bernard?"

"I'm not sure. All I know is that he walked out the front door with his skateboard under his arm."

Twyla and her mother exchanged knowing looks.

"The skateboard, it is a popular sport in America?" Madame Lambert asked.

Mrs. Jones explained to her about skateboards as Twyla ate. Twyla faced the windows and could see Gitano as he lay in the sun. His eyes were closed but his tail flicked at a pesky fly. A hawk circled slowly over the valley, its circle tightening as it zeroed in on some prey below. How lovely to be a hawk and float on air currents like that, Twyla thought. She had almost experienced the thrill once in California when a friend took her hang gliding. But Twyla had lost her nerve at the last moment and was afraid to step off the cliff out into thin air with the heavy winged contraption over her. Instead she had remained earthbound that day, watching the others soar out over the Pacific Ocean and down to the beach below. It looked so easy when others did it, but it was such a big step — that first step of a totally new experience.

Twyla finished her breakfast and went outside to look for Nicholas. She saw him down by the cars at the foot of the stairs. He had found a precious patch of cement there. It was only a small area, with one section built up and out a short distance to meet the dirt road, but it served his purpose well. Twyla sat on the bottom step and watched.

Nicholas went through a routine of intricate maneuvers that Twyla recognized from his last competition at school. He performed the motions slowly but with great precision and style. She watched him and felt proud as he executed a perfect figure eight, then bent forward and did a handstand on his board. As his feet went into the air, the Cross of Lorraine slipped over his head to the ground. He stopped to pick it up, then hopped on the board again, swooped gracefully up the slope to the road's edge, turned, and hot-dogged back to where she sat.

"Very good, Nicky," she said.

"Want a ride?" he asked.

Twyla shook her head. "Not now. I'll just watch for a while."

Her brother continued his tricks on the board and Twyla studied her surroundings. From where she sat she could see the road that came off the highway and continued on up the hill to the left, disappearing behind a turn about fifty feet away. Across the road was a small hill covered with trees and thick underbrush. To either side were more trees and bushes, with some wild flowers dotting the green. How isolated it seemed. How quiet. When the muffled noise of the skateboard's plastic wheels stopped, there was no other sound to be heard except for an occasional bird calling to its mate.

She saw now that the carport was actually an old entrance to the bunker. Someone had bricked up the opening, but the curved retaining walls going into the mountainside were visible. She wondered what level this entrance had led to. Above the carport the hill rose abruptly. There was no visible sign of the bunker beneath its surface.

The sun was warm on Twyla's back but still she shivered. Was it the thought of all those hidden tunnels that chilled her, or the feeling that had come over her a few minutes earlier that they were being watched? She stood and looked all around. There was no sign of anyone in the bushes. But the feeling persisted.

"Where's Bernard?" she asked her brother.

Nicholas shrugged.

"Have you done much exploring around?"

"Nope. Too muddy," was her brother's reply.

Clearly, Nicky was not in a conversational mood.

"How did you sleep?" she asked. But he ignored the question, so she asked, "Did you hear anything last night?"

He stopped for a moment and looked at her. "Why? Did you?"

"I thought I heard something once. Like someone

hammering or tapping."

She had his attention now. He coasted up to her and stopped. "From the tunnel?" he asked.

"I don't know where the sound came from. It was all around me yet seemed to be very far away."

This explanation was too vague for an eight-year-old and he hopped on the board and continued his practice. "Aw, you're just making it up."

"No, I'm not."

"You've been reading too many of those mysteries," he said. "Dad says you have on overactive imagination."

It was obvious to Twyla that Nicholas hadn't heard anything unusual last night. Maybe she had imagined it. Maybe she was also imagining the feeling of being watched now.

A jingling sound behind her made her jump and she turned to see Gitano approaching down the steps. Behind him was Bernard.

Bernard squinted in the sunlight, like a mole venturing out from his hole in the ground. He really needs more fresh air, thought Twyla.

"Hello," he called. "My mother sent me to get you. We are going to the village to drive Marie home and she wants to know if you two want to come along."

Nicholas leaped from his skateboard and ran to join the older boy. Twyla thought if her brother had a tail it would be wagging right now just like Gitano's. She, too, was eager to visit the village of St. Germain, but she rose with a reluctant air so her excitement wouldn't be too obvious. She followed the boys at a distance up the stairs, with Gitano at her heels.

St. Germain was just three miles from the Lamberts' bunker, as you continued on the road they had driven last night. It was a small town, nestled in the gently rolling hills of the area, with vineyards all around. There was one main street of shops, ending at the large square on which stood the village church, the town hall, and a girls' school. From the main street many side streets led up the hill to the vineyards at the top. The houses on these side streets seemed to be built on top of one another.

Marie lived on one of these streets. On the ride into town Twyla had a chance to get acquainted with her. She spoke English, having studied it in school, and she questioned Twyla relentlessly about America. She wanted to know about her home in California and if she knew any film stars. She asked about the American Indians and about Twyla's father's job.

Twyla answered, describing her Spanish-style house in San Diego, overlooking the harbor. She didn't know any movie stars but a friend of hers had once met Rod Stewart. Marie gasped at that information.

Twyla tried to explain that most Indians were not much different from everyone else, at least in San Diego. As for her father's job, she didn't know exactly what work he was doing right now in Frankfurt, but he had been teaching at the university in San Diego before they moved to Germany.

Mrs. Jones supplied information about what the Consulate personnel did in Frankfurt. "They're there to aid Americans who need help in a foreign country," she explained.

Bernard seemed bothered by Marie's questions, feeling perhaps that they were too personal. But Marie, with her good-natured country charm, persisted. Twyla didn't mind. In fact she had a few questions of her own.

She learned that Marie lived with her parents and three younger sisters, who were still in school. Her father worked in the vineyards and her mother helped in the kitchen of a restaurant in town. Twyla had thought Marie was in her late teens when they first met in the bunker. She was surprised when Marie admitted she was just sixteen years old and had been out of school for two years.

"Most people here leave school when they are fourteen," she said.

Bernard sniffed and added, "Unless they are going on to the university."

Bernard obviously was going on to the university, but Twyla didn't think he should have spoken that way to Marie, who was a warm, friendly person. And she was intelligent. She spoke English well and displayed a lot more common sense than Bernard.

But Bernard's attitude didn't seem to bother Marie. The uncomfortable moment passed and Marie chatted on.

Madame Lambert parked her car near the main square and she and Mrs. Jones left the young people to go their own way. They planned to meet in front of the church at noon.

It was market day and stalls had been set up in the square, where the farmers sold their produce to the townspeople. There were great displays of fruit and vegetables, chickens and eggs. One farmer had two pigs for sale and Nicholas paused to study the animals.

"Has he never seen a pig before?" Bernard asked.

"I'm not sure," Twyla answered. "He must have. Though we don't have pigs in the city at home."

In front of the church they encountered a man selling balloons. They were large, brightly colored balloons filled with helium and they floated above the man's head on their individual strings, reaching for the sky. Marie pulled the others toward the vendor and introduced them to him. He was Monsieur Duran, her uncle, the brother of her mother, she explained.

"He has a shop in his house at the edge of town," she said.

"What kind of shop?" Nicholas asked.

"He is an inventor. A tinker. He sells everything and anything."

"Can we go there?" Nicholas asked.

Marie smiled and said, "Of course you can. But on another day. Today his shop is closed, as he will be in the marketplace with his balloons all day."

When they had seen all there was to see in the market Marie led them down the main street.

"I must leave you now but I want to show you where

I live, so that you can visit me someday," she said.

Twyla gazed into the shops they passed. Each one seemed to have its own specialty. There was one that sold only meats. Another was a pharmacy. At the corner was a bakery, with tempting displays of pastries in the window. Marie turned here and beckoned for them to follow her up the steep side street. As they turned the corner Twyla caught sight of a familiar-looking figure leaving the bakery shop. It was the old man they had run into in the rain the night before.

She stopped and watched as he mounted his bicycle and rode away from them, toward the marketplace.

"There's our mysterious stranger in the rain," she cried.

The others stopped and looked at the man on his wobbly bicycle. The basket tied behind him was full of wrapped parcels and two long loaves of French bread stuck out of the top.

"Are you sure?" Bernard asked.

"I would recognize him anywhere," she answered. "Do you know him, Marie?"

Marie said, "No. I have never seen him before. Who is this man?"

Twyla told her about the previous night and about Nicholas's Cross of Lorraine. Then Marie said, "Perhaps Madame Courbet in the bakery shop knows him. Shall we ask?"

The first thing that met Twyla as she entered the shop was the heavenly smell of newly baked bread. It made her mouth water, even though she was not hungry.

Her mother had given Nicky some francs to spend, and he hurried over to a display case and eyed the pastries hungrily.

Bernard and Marie advanced to the counter, but Twyla stood back near the door. The shop was old and dark. The counter tops were of marble, richly sworled in deep pink hues. In one corner was a wrought-iron table and four matching chairs.

Madame Courbet entered from the door at the back. She was a remarkable-looking woman, tall and arrogant. Dressed in black, she wore her black hair pulled back from her face and fastened into a bun. She took her place behind an ornate brass cash register and said *"Bonjour"* and something else in French, which Twyla supposed was the equivalent of "May I help you?"

Bernard spoke in French to Madame Courbet. He asked her about the man who had just left the shop.

Madame Courbet said, "You are mistaken. There was no man here just now."

"But we saw him leave. He was wearing a shabby outer garment of a green color and he rode away on an old bicycle. My friend here recognized him and — " Bernard was interrupted by the woman's abrupt words.

"I know no man of that description. If your friend knows him why do you bother me with these questions?" She looked sharply at Twyla.

Marie, who did business regularly with Madame Courbet, stepped in and said, *"Madame,* pardon us, but we just wanted to return something to him that he left in the Americans' car."

At this Madame Courbet looked alarmed. "Americans? What would that man have to do with Americans?"

"Then there was a man here just now?" said Bernard, smiling in triumph.

"No. I did not say that," the woman said. "I am very busy, children. If that is all you want of me then I must ask you to leave."

She turned her back on them and Marie said, "No. Wait, *madame*." Marie turned to Nicholas, who still had his nose pressed to the glass in front of a selection of napoleons and cherry tarts. "Nicholas, come here. Show Madame Courbet your medal."

Nicholas looked up. "I don't have it," he said.

"But you were wearing it this morning," said Twyla. "I saw it on your neck when you were skateboarding."

"I must have left it in my room when I got ready to come to town," he said.

Twyla understood her brother's reluctance to give up the Cross of Lorraine but she was exasperated with him for not having it with him now.

Marie apologized to the woman for wasting her time and they were about to leave when Nicholas said, "But I want to buy some of these."

Madame Courbet waited on him, taking out of the case two pastries he had selected. She took his money and gave him back some coins in change. Twyla could feel the woman's eyes on them as they left the shop and knew, even before she had gotten the full translation from Bernard, that Madame Courbet was hiding something from them.

44

"Why," she asked, when they stood on the sidewalk outside, "would she deny having seen the man? We know he was in there. His basket was full of bread. And I saw him leave."

"Madame Courbet is a peculiar woman," Marie said. "She is very, how do you say it?, close. Very secretive. Not friendly."

"But she lied to us," said Twyla.

Marie shrugged and Bernard said, "Don't make more of it than there is. She doesn't know the man. Why should she have to tell us any more than that?"

Twyla was silent but her thoughts ran on as they accompanied Marie up the narrow cobbled street to her house. She felt sure Madame Courbet did know the man and that she had been frightened by their questions. Although Twyla did not understand much French, she had understood the woman's attitude well enough.

5

Missing Objects
and Mysterious Noises

"Here is where I live," said Marie as they approached a house near the top of the narrow side street. "Would you like to come in?"

Twyla wanted to, but Bernard said, "We have to get back. It's almost noon and our mothers will be waiting for us."

Twyla cast Marie a helpless look and said, "I guess I had better not today."

"Perhaps you can come again and visit with me?" said Marie.

Twyla said she would like that. When she turned to go she saw that Bernard was already halfway down the street and hadn't even waited to say good-by to Marie.

Twyla said it for him, embarrassed by his lack of manners.

The cobbles were slippery and she had to walk more carefully going down the hill. The boys waited for her at Madame Courbet's shop on the corner, then they walked together to the square.

They all ate lunch at a small café near the church. Afterwards, as they walked back to the car for the drive home, Nicholas, who still had a few coins jingling in his pocket, insisted on making one more purchase before they left.

"It will only take me a minute," he said and he ran toward the church steps.

Twyla could see him hold up his palm to show Marie's uncle how much money he had. Monsieur Duran smiled and nodded and untied a big red balloon from his cart and handed it to the boy. The balloon bobbed around in the back seat all the way to the bunker.

Bernard disappeared into his room as soon as they got home. Nicholas ran off to get his skateboard and Twyla stayed with her mother and Madame Lambert on the deck to enjoy the sunshine. Gitano sat near her, pressing his cold nose against her leg.

Mrs. Jones and Madame Lambert talked. Twyla was amazed that they never seemed to run out of things to say to each other. There was not a lapse in the conversation long enough for her to ask Madame Lambert some questions about Marie and her family. She waited for a lull, but it never came. So she lay back on a deck chair, closed her eyes to the sun, and let her mind wander over the events of the morning and the night before.

She heard Madame Lambert mention that they would be returning to their apartment in Paris when the school term began. The lovely summer home in the bunker would be closed all winter. There was some talk of the Joneses' visiting the Lamberts later in Paris and the thought of that didn't thrill Twyla as much as it should have. Paris was a place she had always dreamed of, but the prospect of seeing it with Bernard didn't appeal to her.

Nicholas joined them and took a seat at the edge of the deck. He tied his balloon to the railing and stared up at it with a melancholy expression on his face. Twyla knew the look. It meant "I am bored. There's nothing to do." And it usually foreshadowed a bout of irritable behavior, when he ceased to be an adorable younger brother and turned into a whining pest.

"Why don't you take your skateboard down to the parking area and practice?" Twyla suggested.

"Because I can't *find* my board," he answered, kicking the deck post in a rhythmic pattern that shook a potted plant nearby, threatening to send it flying to the valley below. He was obviously very angry.

His mother looked at him, sized up the situation, and said, "Nicholas, please don't kick like that. There are miles and miles of open space around for you to run in."

"I want to skateboard," he retorted.

"And he càn't find his board," said Twyla.

"I see," said Mrs. Jones. "Well, it's bound to turn up

48

somewhere. In the meantime, why don't you and Twyla take a walk? Do some exploring."

Nicholas avoided his mother's eyes and mumbled, "Don't want to."

"Well then, how about getting out that model you're working on?"

Mrs. Jones hadn't been in favor of bringing the model on this trip, but Nicholas had promised that if he could have it he would never be bored or troublesome while they were visiting. The look on his face now said that he wasn't in the mood for handwork but that he remembered his promise. He went to get the model.

"He's so full of energy that he must be busy constantly," Mrs. Jones said. "But with all the unexplored territory around here I'm surprised he has nothing to do so early on in our visit."

Madame Lambert nodded. "I know what you mean. The purpose of our spending the summer here was to get Bernard out of doors and healthy again. But here in the country he does just what he does at home. Study. Always he has his nose in his books. I have been busy decorating this old place and consulting with workmen most of the time. It has not been easy to see that he gets enough fresh air. I had hoped that when you came . . ." She paused, then shrugged. Twyla recognized the worried look on her face. She had seen it on her mother's face often enough.

Nicholas returned with the box that held his model and Twyla helped him set up a workbench out on the side yard near the front door. Nicholas unpacked the contents of the box carefully. The look of boredom was replaced by one of new excitement. The dirigible project was the most ambitious he had tried, and each piece he picked from the box received special attention.

The frame and covering of the balloon section were completed and ready to be attached to the cabin. He set this section aside and took out the pieces of the cabin he had yet to finish. There was a moment of panic when he couldn't find the glue, but Twyla found it hidden in the corner of the box under some wads of newspaper.

She watched as he began to work, but soon grew restless and decided to explore the surrounding area. This side yard would be called a patio in California. There was access to the living room of the bunker through large French doors. Near the house was a barbecue, a table, and some chairs for picnics. A grassy area reached out to a stand of trees about twenty feet away. There wasn't a view here as there was from the deck, but Twyla discovered she could see out over the valley from the other side of the trees.

The hill dropped gently from this area and she decided to climb down a short distance so she could get a view of the bunker. Above her she could see the underside of the deck where her mother and Madame Lambert sat. When she walked a little farther down the hill on a diagonal path she had a view of the tower. She stopped, looked back, and studied the hillside fortification from this side.

Only a small portion of the cement walls of the foundation was visible. She could see the windows of their

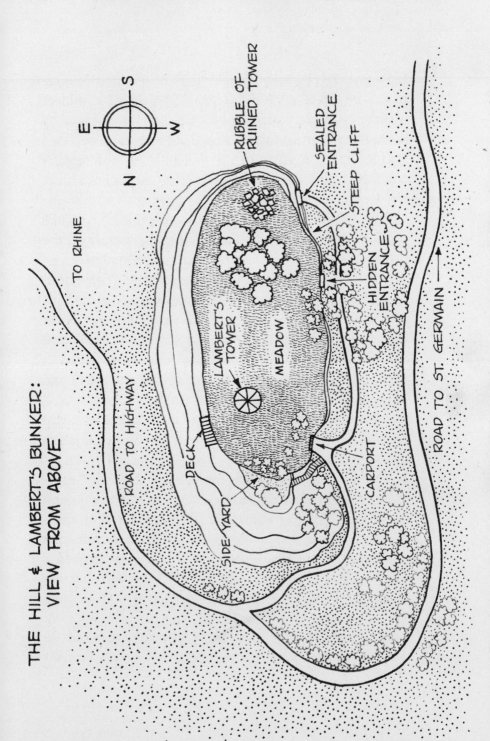

THE HILL & LAMBERT'S BUNKER:
VIEW FROM ABOVE

TO RHINE

ROAD TO HIGHWAY

N
E — W
S

RUBBLE OF
RUINED TOWER

SEALED
ENTRANCE

STEEP CLIFF

HIDDEN
ENTRANCE

MEADOW

LAMBERT'S
TOWER

DECK

SIDE YARD

CARPORT

ROAD TO ST. GERMAIN

bedrooms but nothing below that. The hill took over from there. To the left of her bedroom was a row of more windows covered with rusty steel plates. This was away from the tower and there was no structure above that portion of the bunker — only the hill. She wondered if the bunker extended underground across the entire hill-top.

She climbed back up to the side yard the way she had come. Nicholas didn't look up as she passed through the yard. He was too busy with his project. She noticed he had tied the red balloon to the back of his chair and it bounced gaily in the air above his head as he worked.

Twyla wanted to find a way to get to the top of the hill, so she went down to the road and decided to follow it to see where it led. The road was pleasantly shaded by trees. The country quiet was disturbed only by the twitter of birds and the drone of insects.

The road gently curved at first, so she soon lost sight of the Lamberts' carport. Around the bend a rabbit darted across the road before her. He appeared from behind some logs stacked beside the road on the right. When he saw her he stopped. A few seconds passed while they gazed at each other. Then the rabbit scampered off up the road a few feet before veering to the left and disappearing into the underbrush. Twyla decided to follow him and plunged off the road in pursuit.

Progress was slow. She stopped, heard a faint rustle ahead, and walked toward the sound, pushing aside branches carefully as she went. Just a short way off the road she came to a steep wall of cement built into the side of the hill. The rabbit was not in sight but she felt he must be hidden somewhere, so she turned to the right and followed the wall until it, too, disappeared underground, leaving her at the base of a steep cliff. She realized that she wouldn't get to the top of the hill this way.

She went back to the road and continued her climb. She was in the sunlight now. There were no large trees here, only bushes and a few scrubby pines that didn't look any healthier than Bernard. The road turned to the left, rose sharply, and ended at the side of the hill. Again she found herself facing a steep cliff.

Disappointed at the outcome of her exploration, Twyla turned and walked back to the bunker.

Nicholas waved to her when she reached the yard.

"Come see how much I've done," he cried.

She saw that he had the cabin attached to the balloon section and said, "That's nice, Nicky."

"All I have to do now is put on the propellers and the insignia and I'm done."

The insignia was a special sticker he had made. Instead of "Hindenberg" it read "Nicholas J."

"Ready for your first flight," she said, plopping down on the grass and stretching out on her back.

She stared at the sky and watched a wispy, fair-weather cloud scoot from the west to the east.

"Boy, if I only could," said Nicholas.

"Could what?"

"Fly her," he answered.

He studied the model for a while and then looked at the red balloon straining at the end of its string, as

though it were trying to join the clouds on their east-
ward journey.

"You know, I bet I could fly her. We could have
Marie's uncle fill her with helium and she would fly just
like my balloon."

He gathered up his model and the balloon and ran
toward the front door.

"Where are you going?" Twyla asked.

"To get Bernard. I bet he'll want to help."

That night at the dinner table Nicholas was
all smiles.

"You're in awfully good spirits, Nick," his mother
said. "You must have found your skateboard."

"No, I didn't" he said. "I think someone swiped it."

"Nicholas!" said Mrs. Jones.

Nicholas blushed and stammered. "I mean, I think I
left it down by the road and someone must have come
by and picked it up."

He didn't seem concerned that his prized board had
been stolen. Twyla knew it was because of the dirigible
project.

"What are your plans for launching your blimp?" she
asked.

Bernard, who had ignored the table conversation until
now, said, "It's not a blimp. It's a dirigible. There is a
difference. A dirigible has a rigid frame and a blimp — "

Twyla tossed him a look of exasperation and said,
"You know what I mean."

"The dirigible may not get off the ground," Bernard

said, ignoring her interruption. "I told Nicholas that. I don't think it will hold enough helium to lift the weight."

"It's not that heavy," said Nicholas. He had made up his mind to fly the model and no simple law of physics was going to stop him.

Bernard shrugged. "It's your dirigible," he said.

"We're going to launch her tomorrow. That is, if we can get a ride to town to have Monsieur Duran fill her up with helium for us." He cast a pleading look at his mother.

"I think that can be arranged," his mother answered.

That evening they all sat out on the deck in the twilight and watched the moon rise. Yesterday's storm had washed the air clean and it smelled fresh and sweet, tinged with the odor of wet pines and damp earth. Twyla felt like an eagle in its nest sitting above the silent valley under the ever darkening sky, with only the occasional voice of a forest creature breaking the silence far below them. Way off in the distance a light flickered, probably from a boat on the Rhine.

Bernard excused himself early and went to his room. Nicholas fell asleep on a lounge chair and they let him rest until Twyla went down to her room. She felt sleepy, too, and there were no disturbing thoughts of spooky tunnels tonight. She fell asleep immediately.

She awoke once and heard the clink of Gitano's collar in the hall outside, followed by the closing of a door. Probably her mother going to bed, she thought, and she turned over and went back to sleep.

It was much later when she awoke again, this time from a dream. She had dreamed she was on a road and at every turn she ran into a blank wall. She was afraid in her dream, too. She wasn't sure just what the menace was, but it seemed imperative that she get away from it.

She lay awake thinking of her dream and wondering what it meant. Dreams usually meant something, she knew. This one wasn't hard to figure out. It was obviously caused by her experience on the road today, when she was looking for a way to the top of the hill but kept running into dead ends.

As Twyla lay in that state between wakefulness and sleep she heard a noise and felt her muscles, so relaxed before, tense up. The noise sounded like a groan. She couldn't tell which direction it came from. It could have come in through her open window, but the valley was so far below that a sound from that direction did not seem possible. Her mother's window was probably open, too, but this groan was too deep to have been made by a woman, or by her brother, in his room. Bernard's room was too far above her for his voice to have reached her here.

From her afternoon walk Twyla knew that the openings to more gun emplacements were not far from her own window, and she decided that the sound must have come from there — if there had been a sound. She wasn't even sure she had heard the sound, because now her room was as quiet as a tomb.

But her doubts vanished when another noise reached

her. It sounded like something being dragged across a floor. Then there was another groan. Then silence.

Twyla heard nothing more after that, although she lay awake listening for a long time before finally falling asleep. When she again opened her eyes the sun was streaming into her room and all feelings of menace had gone with the night.

6

A Long-Ago Tragedy

Everyone had eaten by the time Twyla got to the breakfast table. A place had been set for her and she saw the basket of fresh croissants and bread that meant that Marie had gotten there already. Twyla hoped she hadn't missed her French friend by rising so late.

A few minutes later Marie bustled into the room, a dry mop in her hands. She headed for the kitchen but stopped when she saw Twyla.

"Bonjour," she said. "How are you today?"

"Bonjour, Marie," Twyla answered. "I wish I felt as peppy as you look."

Marie's face showed concern. "You have not slept well?" she asked.

Twyla shook her head. "Not well at all. Sit down and let me tell you why."

Marie, clutching the mop, stood firm. "No. I mustn't."

"It's all right. Have you had breakfast?"

"Yes. A long time ago."

"Then just sit and keep me company while I eat."

Marie took a seat at one end of the table, though she did not look very comfortable about it.

"What has happened, Twyla?" she asked.

"I heard strange noises from below last night," Twyla answered as she spooned a large dollop of plum preserves onto a piece of French bread. "I'm sure someone was down there. Either that or . . ."

Marie waited for the alternative, holding her breath.

"Or ghosts," said Twyla.

"*Mon Dieu!*" Marie exclaimed.

At that moment Bernard clattered down the spiral staircase near the kitchen and walked into the dining area. Marie jumped up from the table and began pushing the mop around the edges of the rug. Bernard seemed to be in extra-good spirits this morning. His eyes had a spark in them that Twyla hadn't seen before. He looked at Twyla and then toward the busy Marie.

"Am I interrupting?" he asked.

"I was just telling Marie that I heard strange noises again last night," she said. "From the bunker."

The spark left Bernard's eyes as he lowered a grim look her way. "It was just your imagination," he said.

"Or a dream." He started for the living room, then stopped.

"Did you say 'again'?" he asked.

"Yes. The night before, I heard something too. But last night's noise was different. I definitely heard someone groan. And then it sounded like something was being pulled across a floor. A sliding noise. Oh, it's hard to describe just what I heard, because it all seemed so far away and unreal."

"And the night before?" Bernard asked. "What did you hear then?"

Twyla attacked her egg, peeling the shell off carefully as she talked. She rather enjoyed relating a spooky story by day. It was more fun than living through one at night.

"The night before, it was more like someone tapping on metal. And it seemed much farther away than the groans I heard last night."

Bernard came back to the table and sat in the chair Marie had just vacated.

"Did you, uh, investigate this sound?" he asked. He seemed much more interested than he had a moment before. But it wasn't an excited interest, like Marie's. His was more the cold-blooded, get-to-the-bottom-of-it type of interest.

"No, I didn't investigate," Twyla answered. "If you must know, I was scared. Too scared to even open my eyes."

She expected him to laugh at her. He didn't. He just nodded his head.

Marie stepped forward and said, "Perhaps it was a

ghost. There is talk of such things in the district."

"There is?" Bernard asked.

"Oh, yes. It is nothing new. My grandmother used to tell us stories of the ghosts of Roman soldiers who roam these hills — especially near the vineyards."

"What would a Roman ghost be doing around here?" Twyla asked.

Bernard explained. "Many of the vineyards date from Roman times. Didn't you know?"

"How could I? I haven't been here two days yet," Twyla said defensively. She wondered how he always managed to make her feel like a know-nothing.

Marie continued. "Yes, the Romans settled in this area long ago. My grandmother says some people still see a lost legion wandering over the hills. They moan and cry out in great agony for their homeland. There is also the ghost of a young girl who haunts the village. She was martyred by the Romans. Her relics are in the church, encased in the cross. You can see the bones through a little glass door on the front of the cross."

Bernard sneered. "Peasant superstition!" he said.

"Oh, no. It is a true story." Marie turned to Twyla and said, "I will show you today. *Mon Dieu!* I have forgotten to tell you. You are invited to come to my home for lunch today. Then I will show you the whole town. Your mother says it is all right for you to come. That is, if you want to. "

"I'd love to," said Twyla.

"Good," said Marie. She resumed her mopping job and said, "I must finish this now."

Bernard stood to leave. His attitude had changed again and he said, "Maybe it was a ghost you heard, Twyla. I wouldn't go wandering around alone if I were you." Then he left them.

"What do you make of that boy?" Twyla asked.

"What do you mean?" Marie asked.

"At first he was very interested in the noises I heard. Then he laughed at the idea of your ghosts. Then, just now, he said maybe there are ghosts here." Twyla shook her head. "I just don't understand him at all."

"He has, how would you say?, many parts," said Marie. "He is not very happy, I think."

Twyla finished off the last of the croissants and said, "You are much more generous in your opinions than I, Marie."

An hour later Mrs. Jones drove the young people to the village. Madame Lambert stayed at the bunker. She was expecting an electrician to do some work on their generator.

Marie directed them first to her uncle's shop, on the far side of St. Germain. The shop was attached to his house, in what had once been a barn. Monsieur Duran was working on a solar-energy system, which interested them immediately.

"We could use a system like this at the bunker," Bernard said.

Monsieur Duran showed them how it worked. Bernard, Twyla, and Nicholas listened intently, while Marie translated for the Americans.

"He is happy to have visitors," Marie said. "Not many come out here. He is not a successful businessman. People say he is too fanciful. Is that a good word?"

"That is a very good word," Mrs. Jones said. "I think your uncle has a very inventive mind and is perhaps too visionary for the average man. Many inventors are like that. But at least he is happy in his work."

"Oh, yes. He is that," Marie agreed. "And he makes a small living selling his balloons at fairs and on market day. He also does odd jobs for people."

Bernard said, "I will tell my mother about him. We are always having breakdowns in the electrical system and there are many other jobs to be done around the bunker. Maybe next summer, when we return from Paris, we can plan a solar system for the bunker. It would be nice to have a good supply of hot water for showers even when the generator goes out."

Monsieur Duran was pleased with the prospect of future work for the Lamberts.

A half-hour had passed before Nicholas remembered the original purpose of his visit. He held up the dirigible model for Monsieur Duran to see and Bernard explained that they wanted to fill it with helium so they could fly it.

While Monsieur Duran studied the problem Twyla inspected the shop and its curious contents. One corner was devoted to bicycle repairs. There was a stack of parts and tools on a table, and several bikes were in various stages of repair. Marie explained that her uncle salvaged old models, restored them, and sold them at the marketplace.

Monsieur Duran also worked on clocks. One wall was covered with clocks of all shapes, sizes, and vintages. About half of them were working and at eleven o'clock the visitors were treated to a symphony of gongs, chimes, and cuckoos — a cacophony that Twyla found delightful.

Nicholas got his dirigible filled as he wanted, and he also got a short lecture, translated by Bernard, on the physics of air flight. Monsieur Duran suggested that an auxiliary balloon might be necessary to get the dirigible off the ground. He gave Nicholas a balloon for that purpose and wished him luck, making the young people promise they would return to his shop to tell him how the flight had gone.

A short time later Mrs. Jones dropped Marie and Twyla off at the corner near the bakery shop, and then she and the boys returned to the bunker. Marie's father, Monsieur Beury, would drive Twyla home later that afternoon, when he returned from the vineyards.

Before climbing the hill to Marie's house, the girls stopped at the bakery, where Marie purchased a long loaf of bread. If Madame Courbet remembered their confrontation of the day before she did not show it. She waited on them with the cool air of a polite though distant stranger. On the short climb to Marie's house Twyla commented on the woman's behavior.

Marie nodded and said, "The French sometimes prefer to ignore unpleasant situations. And Madame Courbet has many to ignore."

"How is that?"

"I mentioned to my mother her curious behavior and my mother told me something of Madame Courbet's past. Much of it is very sad."

Twyla listened with interest as Marie recounted the woman's history. Madame Courbet had not always lived in this town. Before the Second World War she had lived in a small village just across the Rhine. She married a young man from St. Germain and moved here. Then in the early years of the war her husband was killed. They had no children, but Madame Courbet had a younger sister, Theresa, who lived with her because their parents were dead.

It was rumored that Theresa worked in the French Underground throughout the war, which did not please Madame Courbet, since the two women were German by birth. Nevertheless, Madame Courbet protected her sister from the Gestapo, the Nazi police, making it very dangerous for both of the sisters. Madame Courbet owned a small restaurant that catered to the district Gestapo, who liked her German cooking.

In this part of France, Marie explained, there were, and still are, many people who feel more kinship with Germany than with France. The border has changed so many times through the wars. At any rate, half the townspeople condemned Madame Courbet for her association with the German soldiers. Only a few people knew of her sister's work in the Underground.

"Where is Madame Courbet's sister now?" Twyla asked.

"Ah, that is the sad part of the story," said Marie.

65

"During the war Theresa fell in love with and married a man named Charles LaVesque, who also worked in the Underground. His family had emigrated to America many years before. He was raised in America but spoke French like a native and could pass for French. He came back here to work as a liaison between the French and the Americans.

"Before the Germans were pushed back across the Rhine, Theresa and her husband were killed by the Nazis."

"How terrible!" said Twyla.

"They were only two of many," said Marie. "During the war there was much suffering and bloodshed all around. My mother says that Madame Courbet has never been the same since that time. She has few friends in the district. My mother tries to be nice to her always. That is why my mother knows more than most people about the sad events here.

"Each month Madame Courbet goes to the grave of her sister and leaves flowers. It is a long trip for her, because she does not have an automobile. My father drives her sometimes, when his business with the vineyards takes him that way."

Twyla found that her opinion of Madame Courbet had altered now that she knew more of the woman's past.

Marie broke into her thoughts with the announcement "Here we are."

7

Roman Ghosts
and Brynna

Twyla had been so engrossed in the story of Madame Courbet's past that she hadn't noticed the steep climb on slippery cobblestones to Marie's house. She now followed Marie up the three steps to the front door and into the dark wood-paneled hallway she had glimpsed the day before.

Marie led the way down the hall to the back of the house. The last room was the kitchen, off the hall to the right. It was a bright room, thanks to two large windows that looked out on the small garden in back. Copper utensils hung over an ancient black stove in one corner. A large table with a marble top stood in the center of the room. Though the room and furnishings were old, everything was sparkling clean and orderly.

Twyla stood at the sink by the windows looking out to the yard and said, "In a kitchen like this I think doing the dishes would be almost fun."

Marie laughed.

There was a picnic basket on the counter. Marie looked inside and said, *"Bon.* Maman has prepared our lunch already, so we have nothing to do but enjoy ourselves."

"A picnic?" Twyla asked.

"You like picnics?"

Twyla nodded.

"Good. I do, too. And we can see some of St. Germain at the same time."

They left the house a few minutes later with the picnic basket swinging between them. Marie led the way up the hill to what Twyla had thought was a dead end. An old stone stairway was set in the wall at the top of the street. They took the stairs, and at the top, Twyla had the first surprise of the afternoon.

The brow of the hill was terraced and planted in grapevines. The plantings extended over and down the other side, away from the village, and the view from both sides of the hill was spectacular. On one side were the tiled roofs of St. Germain, the spires of the church, and something Twyla had not seen before, a canal running through the town near the marketplace in the square.

On the other side was the vineyard. It extended all the way to the valley and beyond, with more hills and vineyards as far as she could see.

Marie pointed to a wooded area to the northeast and said, "There is the hill with the Lamberts' bunker. And beyond, though you cannot see from here, are the Rhine and Germany."

Twyla felt as if she were standing on top of the world. "I'd like to stay here forever," she said with a sigh.

"Don't you miss your home?" Marie asked.

"We have moved so much because of Daddy's work that I don't have any one home," Twyla answered. "I've had many homes, and one or two friends in each place, whom I still write to. Just when I'm getting used to a new school we're off again. Daddy tells me I have the best of all worlds, but sometimes I wonder what it would be like to live in just one town for ever and ever, as you are living here in St. Germain."

Marie shuddered. "I hope I don't have to live here for ever and ever," she said.

"You don't want to stay here?"

"No. I long to go to Paris and work in a fashionable dress shop on the Champs Élysées."

Twyla jumped up and down. "Oh, good!" she said. "And when I am an elegant lady, a sophisticated woman of the world, I will come to you and buy all my clothes!" She pranced around Marie in her best "elegant lady" fashion. Then she collapsed in giggles on the ground and said, "Of course, you will have to carry a special line for elegant ladies who are only five feet two inches tall."

"But of course," said Marie. "Many ladies in France are your height."

"They are? Boy, they sure aren't in California. Everything I buy has to be taken up. My mother got tired of doing it and now I have to do the hemming myself. What a chore!" She grimaced, then asked, "Can we eat right here? It's so lovely on this hill."

"There is a better place a little farther on," said Marie.

Twyla followed Marie to a spot just a short walk away. The view was about the same but here, under a grape arbor, were a wooden table and benches for their picnic. Vines clinging to the arbor shaded them from the hot midday sun. A breeze whispered through the leaves, and overhead, just an arm's length away, hung clumps of ripe Burgundy-colored grapes.

"Can we pick these?" Twyla asked.

"If you wish," Marie said. "Though they are not quite right for eating."

Twyla tried one anyway. It was a little too tart for her taste but she enjoyed being able to reach up and pick the fruit off the vine. At home they had a tangerine tree and a peach tree in their yard, but she had never picked grapes before.

Marie opened the basket and removed a red-and-white checkered cloth, which she spread out on the table. Onto this she arranged their lunch. There was bread with thick slices of ham, and cheese of two varieties, one yellow and one white. There were plums and apricots for dessert and two bottles of a soft drink with the name on the label, which Twyla found impossible to pronounce. Marie said it for her and it sounded like "psst." Both girls laughed at Twyla's attempt to imitate her and then they settled down to enjoy their meal.

As they ate, Marie pointed out the various sights in the town below. Almost directly below was Marie's street, at the end of which was Madame Courbet's shop. To the left of that, almost in the center of town, were the church and the square. Behind ran the blue ribbon of water, the canal, that disappeared between two hills at the far end of town.

"Near there is my uncle's place," said Marie. "And beyond are only a few farms and then the Vosges Mountains."

Twyla munched on the chewy French-style *jambon*, or ham, sandwich, and gazed at the picturesque scene. It looked like a toy town with miniature houses and model trees. It reminded her of pictures she had seen as a child in her fairy-tale books.

"It looks so different from here," she said. "It is truly beautiful."

Marie beamed. "It is nice. But America is nice also, is it not?"

"Oh, yes. But in a different way. We have nothing like this in San Diego." She pointed down to the hodge-podge of roofs below that formed a jumble of patterns and levels. "And nothing at home is as old as this. For example, we do not have ghosts of Roman soldiers marching over our hills."

Twyla looked down to the other side of the hill and asked, "Is this where the lost legion marches?"

Marie said it was and Twyla felt a little chill along her spine.

"Have you ever seen them?" she asked.

"No. But sometimes, in the middle of the night, I hear the wind moaning over this hill and it is easy to imagine them."

"Does it frighten you?"

"No," said Marie simply. "It makes me sad sometimes to think of the poor lost souls."

"I'm not afraid of most things, such as animals or high places," said Twyla. "But ghosts scare me."

"I am just the opposite," said Marie. "The dead cannot hurt you, but the real live dangers of this world can."

They finished eating and packed the empty bottles and dishes into the basket. On their way to town they left the basket at Marie's house then walked into the heart of St. Germain. Marie chose streets that Twyla had not yet seen, some only a few feet wide in places, with old houses of stone rising up steeply on both sides, so that the sun never reached the pavement. Marie pointed out interesting local artifacts, such as the long marble troughs, filled with water, on some street corners.

"For the animals to drink from," she explained. "They are old sarcophagi, or burial boxes, dug up from the ground by farmers. They are Roman."

At last they reached the church and Twyla watched as Marie took out two scarves from a pocket. She put one on her own head and handed the other to Twyla. Inside the church, Marie dipped her fingers in a bowl of water and made the sign of the cross, touching her forehead, heart, and both shoulders. Twyla was not Catholic but she did as Marie had done.

They walked down a side aisle of the church to a place near the altar. The stone floor was worn uneven from the many worshipers who had been here in the last seven hundred years. Twyla was amazed that a building so old was still standing and still felt so solid and protective.

Streams of yellow sunlight shown on them in the front pew from the clerestory windows high in the church walls. Where the sun did not reach, the church was in shadows, except for one corner where a bank of lighted candles burned. Candles had been placed there by people who prayed for special favors or blessings for their friends or relatives.

On the altar before them was a golden cross. In the center of the cross was a window. Twyla could see something inside but could not distinguish what it was.

"Inside the cross are the bones of the girl who haunts the village," explained Marie in a hushed voice. "Her name was Brynna. She was a peasant girl of the district, blonde and blue-eyed, like you."

Then Marie told Twyla that Brynna had been the pride of her mother and father. The family was Christian at a time when many Romans still worshiped the old gods. Christianity was spreading, especially among the peasants and slaves, who responded to its message of peace and love and equality before God.

As Brynna grew to an age when she appealed to men, her parents and friends feared for her safety and hid her from the Roman soldiers as well as they could. But one day when Brynna went to the well to draw water, a group of soldiers captured her and took her to their camp. She escaped but was killed during her flight.

It was said that she forgave her abductors before her last breath of life, and the soldiers repented and buried her with great honor.

"It is not known," said Marie, "when the bones were placed in the cross. Many parts of the legend are not known. But my grandmother told us the story as she had heard it from her mother."

"But you say she is now seen as a ghost?" Twyla asked.

"My grandmother said there have been encounters with her. Usually on a dark road at night, or in a quiet place, and usually when the person involved faces a great crisis. Brynna appears in a white dress with a blue mantle over her head. She remains for a moment and then is gone. It is said that the sight of Brynna brings luck and an end to one's troubles. For that reason, many people through the ages have believed she should be elevated to sainthood. But the case has not been documented sufficiently and it remains just a lovely legend."

As they sat in the empty church Twyla could almost see Brynna, so vivid was the story as Marie told it. In these surroundings, remote from the hurry and cares of the world outside, it was easy to believe in ghosts.

At last Marie stood and said, "We must go. My father will be home by now and will be waiting to drive you back to the bunker."

They walked up a side aisle to the back of the church.

As they neared the curtained confessional they heard the sound of footsteps entering the church. Marie touched Twyla's arm and pointed to the woman who had come in and was walking toward the altar. It was Madame Courbet.

They watched as she kneeled at the altar and bowed her head in prayer. A moment later she stood up again and moved toward the corner where the votive candles glowed. She put an offering in a nearby box then took a new candle, lit it, and placed it with the others on the tall stand against the wall.

The girls hadn't meant to spy on her but they watched as though mesmerized. Suddenly Madame Courbet turned and walked up the side aisle directly toward them. Twyla was embarrassed and she could tell that Marie felt the same way. Marie pulled her back through a curtain and into the confessional.

They waited for Madame Courbet to pass. Marie was pressed up against the back of the booth and Twyla's nose touched the curtain in front. It was hot and stuffy in the confined space. Twyla could smell the dust from the curtain and her nose began to itch. She pulled an edge of the scarf up over her nose and prayed she wouldn't sneeze.

Madame Courbet's footsteps stopped. The next thing Twyla knew the curtain was pushed back and she stood face to face with the woman. A shaft of sunlight from above and across the church blinded Twyla momentarily, and she blinked, aware only of the silhouette of the woman before her.

Twyla thought she must say something, but she was too frightened and embarrassed to do so. She heard Madame Courbet gasp. Then the woman crossed herself quickly and the curtain fell between them again. Twyla and Marie stood motionless as the sound of Madame Courbet's footsteps died away.

Twyla turned to Marie and said, "I think we frightened her. Oh Marie, I am so ashamed. How will we ever be able to face her again after this? Now she thinks we were spying on her."

Marie shook her head and said, "No. She couldn't see me at all. And your face was half hidden by the scarf. She did not recognize you, I am sure. But I think . . . I think . . ."

"What, Marie?"

Marie's voice was barely a whisper when she continued. "I think Madame Courbet has just been visited by the ghost of Brynna, the peasant girl."

8

The Flight of the *Nicholas J.*

There was very little conversation between Twyla and Marie's father on the drive to the bunker. Marie had stayed home, since her father, Monsieur Beury, would not be returning to the village until late. He spoke little English. This left Twyla alone with her thoughts.

She would have preferred conversation. Her thoughts were disturbing ones, owing to the encounter with Madame Courbet in the church. Marie had told her that the shaft of sunlight from the church windows had shone on Twyla's head, making it the one bright spot in the shadowy confessional. The blond hair that showed from beneath the scarf had glistened like a gold halo in the light. Marie said if she had been Madame Courbet, she, too, would have mistaken Twyla for an apparition.

All this talk of ghosts, Roman soldiers marching over vineyards, and young girls appearing in dark corners had unnerved Twyla. She was relieved to be going back to a bunker that was only fifty years old instead of fifteen hundred years old. It had been a marvelous day almost to the very end, but she knew that end was going to haunt her until she thought of a way to explain the incident in the church to Madame Courbet.

Nicholas and Bernard were working on the dirigible when Twyla reached the side yard at the bunker. Gitano ran to greet her, his bushy tail wagging rapidly. She could hear her mother's and Madame Lambert's lively talk through the open patio doors. Everything seemed normal again and Twyla was glad to be back.

"You're just in time for the launching," Nicholas's excited voice called to her.

"I'll be right out," she said, ducking into the living room to tell her mother she had returned.

When she came back to the yard Bernard was positioning a ladder against the bunker near the sliding doors of the patio area.

"What's that for?" she asked.

"To get to the top of the hill," said Nicholas.

Bernard held the ladder and said, "You can go first and I will hold it for you."

Twyla saw the frown on his face and replied, "You won't have to hold it on my account. I'm not afraid to climb ladders."

78

Bernard looked disappointed, shrugged, and scrambled up the ladder. At the top he disappeared into a thick vine above the windows. He poked his head out and said to Nicholas, "O.K. Hand me the dirigible."

Nicholas climbed up part way, handed over his precious model, then completed the climb, and he too disappeared.

It was Twyla's turn. She was a good climber but still she made it a point not to look down. At the top she scooted through the vine and discovered she was on the flat overhang that formed part of the new roof of the family room. Just a few feet away the hill began, rising in a gentle slope that she could handle easily. And then, suddenly, she was where she had tried to be the day before — on the top of the hill.

The bunker tower a short distance away rose two stories high. The windows from Bernard's room were about twenty feet off the ground, but at ground level Twyla saw the remains of an old door.

"It's been sealed off," Bernard said. "But I'm going to see if my mother will allow me to have it opened again."

The top of the hill was nearly flat, with scattered bushes. Grass, ankle-deep and summer-dry, grew here now. Bernard said that they let a local shepherd graze his flock here to keep the grass down.

Rocky outcrops were scattered about and in the distance was a stand of trees. Twyla had been able to see those trees from the end of the road the day before. She longed to go there immediately and investigate that part of the hill, but Bernard had started to prepare a launch pad near the tower, so she stayed to watch.

Bernard knelt at the chosen spot, holding the dirigible and balloon to the ground, while Nicholas checked the string to make sure it was tied securely.

"How much string do you have, Nicky?" she asked.

"Five hundred feet," he answered, patting his hip pocket. "It's the new fishing line Dad gave me for my birthday. Good and strong."

When both boys had made sure the connections were right, Nicholas took the roll of string from his pocket and began to unwind it, walking backwards as he did.

"O.K. Let 'er go!" he yelled.

Bernard let go and the dirigible popped up into the air to a height of about ten feet. Nicholas grinned as he watched his airship bob on the end of the string, straining toward the clear blue sky. Twyla and Bernard cheered and Nicholas began slowly to unwind more string.

Up and up it went, looking like a real dirigible flying high over their heads. A breeze rippled through the grass and the model drifted off toward the trees, away from the tower. Nicholas played on the string as if a trout were on the end of his line, coaxing it, teasing it. The wind at the higher level was strong, causing the ship to drift dangerously close to the trees. Bernard and Twyla ran in that direction, keeping themselves under the model.

"You'd better reel her in a little," Bernard said.

The dirigible dipped erratically.

"The balloon's popped!" Bernard cried.

THE HILL: WEST ELEVATION

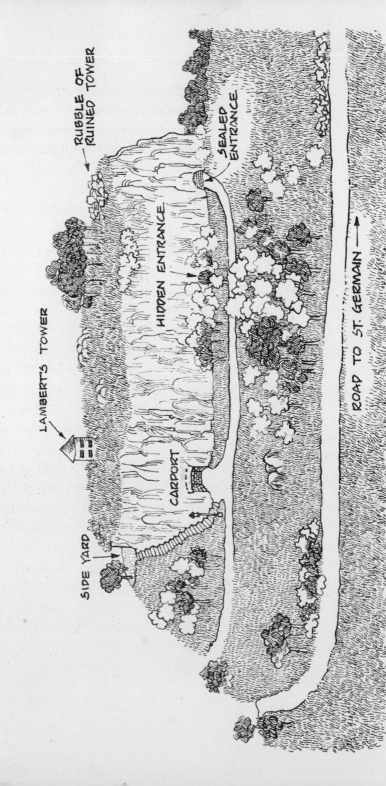

RUBBLE OF RUINED TOWER

SEALED ENTRANCE

HIDDEN ENTRANCE

LAMBERT'S TOWER

CARPORT

SIDE YARD

ROAD TO ST. GERMAIN →

"Nicky, reel it in. Hurry," said Twyla.

The younger boy wound the string as fast as he could. Twyla prayed that the dirigible wouldn't fall into the trees. Bernard sprang forward, grabbed the string, and helped pull as Nicholas continued to wind it on the wooden form. They weren't quick enough. The dirigible dipped low over the trees and disappeared. The string became caught and they couldn't pull it in.

By this time all three children were just a short distance from the trees. They ran the rest of the way.

"Keep winding," Bernard called, as he ran under the first tree.

Twyla followed, looking up into the branches, trying to see where the dirigible had landed. The string had hooked onto high branches in the nearest tree. Bernard told Nicholas to tie the roll of string securely to the trunk of the tree, which the young boy did. Then they tried to follow the string with their eyes. It led them through the small grove to the clearing on the other side.

"Oh, no!" cried Twyla.

Before them was an immense formation of rocks and blocks of cement lying in a jumbled mass on the edge of the hill. Beyond was a steep drop off to the valley below.

Bernard climbed a large chunk of cement and picked up the end of the string, which lay limp across the rocks. The dirigible was gone.

"The string broke," he said. "Probably cut off by one of these jagged edges."

Nicholas looked as though he was about to cry and Twyla put an arm around his shoulders.

"Don't worry, Nicky," she said. "We'll find it. It must be somewhere nearby."

Nicholas shook his head. "It flew away," he said. "It will probably keep on going until it gets to Germany."

"Maybe not," she answered. "If the auxiliary balloon burst, then the model was on its way down when the string broke. It couldn't have gone far."

She looked out at the view. From this end of the hill she could see the canal leading to the village of St. Germain and the terraced vineyards beyond. The distant village rooftops shimmered in the late-afternoon sun. Above them she could see where she and Marie had had their picnic. The land between here and there was wooded. She realized that the possibility of finding Nicholas's airship in that countryside was hopeless, but if the model had touched down on this hill there was a chance they might find it.

She looked around her at the huge rock pile. The task of finding it here was not going to be that easy, either.

"What is this, anyway?" she asked Bernard.

"Looks like a dynamited tower," Bernard answered. "Maybe it was another entrance to the bunker at one time."

"Do you think it was bombed?" Nicholas asked.

Bernard shrugged. "Could be. But then again it could have been done after the war. For a time people tried to salvage some of the steel holding these places together.

They gave up, though. It was too big a job to dynamite all that concrete."

They scrambled along from block to block, avoiding the rusted ribbons of twisted steel that lay among the boulders.

"We'll never find anything in this mess," said Nicholas. "We might as well give up."

The boys started back toward the trees. Twyla sat on a large lump of concrete and thought about the tower that once stood here. If there was a tower, it meant that below this jumble of rock and concrete were more tunnels and caverns like the ones under the Lamberts' tower — somewhere below her feet, she thought, looking down.

A patch of color wedged in between the rocks caught her eye and she bent over to pick it up. It was all that remained of the red auxiliary balloon.

At dinner that night the young people told their mothers of the afternoon's adventure, of the dirigible's disappearance, and about their discovery of the dynamited tower on the far edge of the hill.

Madame Lambert listened to their report and said, "Bernard's father did mention another tower on the property. When he bought this piece of land he was given a tour of the place. And Bernard is right. A salvage firm did try to take some of the metal out, but it was too big a job. Too expensive. The blasting they did destroyed that portion of the bunker and you must promise me you will not play there. It is too dangerous. If there are more tunnels over there, they will be in no condition for safe exploration."

Mrs. Jones said, "It sounds as though you had an exciting afternoon. I'm sorry about your model, Nicholas. But you can always build another one."

Nicholas, still brooding, nodded and said, "You should have seen her fly, Mom. It was beautiful."

"I'm sure it was," she answered.

Nicholas yawned all through dinner and went to bed early. In spite of the disappointment of losing the dirigible, it had been a thrilling and tiring day for him. Twyla sat up late by the fire, reading a mystery. Bernard retired to his room early, as usual.

Twyla and her mother went down to their rooms at eleven o'clock. Twyla still wasn't sleepy. She had reached an exciting part of the book and wanted to finish it. She changed into her pajamas, snuggled into the comfortable bed, propped herself up against her pillows, and lost herself in the story.

She was still reading at midnight when she heard the clinking of Gitano's collar in the hall outside her door. Distracted from the story, she became aware of another sound, much like the one she had heard the night before.

All the fears she had forgotten came rushing back to her as she listened. Then she thought, if Gitano was outside her door there was nothing to fear. She didn't really believe in ghosts. And if the sounds came from a human or animal source, then Gitano would protect her.

She got out of bed, put on her robe, and slipped her feet into her sneakers. The hall was dark but the light from her room illuminated it enough for her to see. Gitano was lying near the end of the hall by the big steel door. He lifted his head when he saw her and his tail slapped against the floor.

The steel door was slightly ajar. From the opening Twyla heard the ghostly sound of an object being dragged across a floor. It sounded far away — not so far as last night, but then she hadn't ventured out into the hall last night. The sound definitely came from beyond the steel door: from the tunnels in the unoccupied part of the bunker.

As she stood listening, Gitano laid his huge head back down on the floor. If Gitano wasn't concerned then she shouldn't be.

She heard a thud and a groan. The groan echoed eerily through the hall and she shivered involuntarily. Gitano lifted his head again and then stood and peered through the crack in the door. Even he seemed concerned now, and Twyla fought the impulse to run and hide in her nice warm bed until morning, as she had done the night before.

She did not run to her bed. Instead, she grabbed the flashlight from her dresser then went back to the hallway and crept forward toward the end of it. Gitano stood ready at her side as she put her shoulder against the cold steel door and slowly pushed it open.

9

One Mystery Solved

Before her stretched a deep, empty chamber. On the left were windows like those in the bedrooms — gun emplacements. But here there were no interior walls separating them. This must be what the bedroom area had looked like before the Lamberts partitioned it, Twyla thought as she shone the beam of her flashlight around the cavernous room.

To the right was a stairway leading down. She caught sight of the tip of Gitano's tail as it disappeared around the first curve. An eerie light illuminated the stairwell and she crept toward it.

On a wall below she saw a strange dancing shadow. It swayed back and forth in a menacing manner and stretched its arms to the side. As she watched, fascinated, she saw it rise up in the air, then disappear. A loud, painful groan followed. The groan echoed all around her, bouncing off the walls in the deep recesses of the bunker.

Twyla was no longer afraid, for at that instant she realized what it was. She knew Gitano was down there, and though he was a friendly dog, she knew he would not go readily to a stranger.

She tiptoed down the stairs and stood at the bottom, at the entrance to another large cavern. This one was like the room above but had no windows. A single light suspended from the ceiling lit the room. The walls and ceiling were of cement. At the opposite side of the room was another doorway, opened to a dark area. She shivered at the thought of more passageways beyond, unlit and unexplored. But her attention focused on the scene in the room before her.

Bernard was there with Gitano. The dog sat to one side, away from his master, who had one foot on Nicholas's skateboard and was preparing to push off for a run over the smooth concrete. The dragging sound filled the air. Why hadn't she recognized it before? she wondered. It was the muted sound of plastic skate wheels against cement. She had heard it all her life, it seemed, but of course never before had she heard it coming from an underground fortress and bouncing off scores of cement walls.

Now she waited for that other frightening sound — the groan. This she would enjoy. She found herself smiling in anticipation of what would happen inevitably.

It was not a long wait. Bernard had pushed off with

his right foot and, struggling to maintain his balance, had put that foot up on the board. His form was all wrong. His back arched, his arms flew out, and the skateboard went flying as he flipped off into the air and landed with a thud on the floor.

"Ouch," said Twyla, walking into the room. "That must have hurt."

Bernard, with difficulty, suppressed a groan. He looked up at her, startled.

"What are you doing here?" he asked, an angry flash in his eyes.

"Ghost hunting," she answered. "Something you tried to discourage me from doing with all your talk this morning."

He picked himself up off the floor, avoiding her gaze.

"So this is why Nicky's skateboard disappeared," she said. Before he could answer she moved toward the board near the dark opening on the other side of the room. "Watch how it's done," she said, hopping on the board with a nimble grace learned after many mistakes years before.

Twyla executed a few simple turns. She decided not to try anything too fancy. It had been a few years since she was the girl terror of Jackdaw Street, and she didn't want to lose her advantage over Bernard now that she had him in a compromising position. She used the full length of the room as she skated. It was a perfect place for skateboarding.

"You ought to tell Nicholas about this," she said. "It's a great practice room."

"I intended to," Bernard answered. "But I thought I'd . . . I would . . ."

"Practice a little first?" she volunteered. "It helps to have someone show you the fine points. You could have asked him."

Bernard didn't answer. He looked miserable, as if he wished the floor would open up and swallow him.

She continued. "Were you watching us that first morning?" she asked, remembering the feeling she'd had of being watched. The expression on his face told her he had been.

He turned to leave and said, "It's a silly sport, anyway."

"Wait. Don't leave me down here all alone," she said. Her moment of glory was gone and she discovered that it hadn't been as satisfying as she had hoped. She had thought that finding Bernard with Nicholas's missing skateboard and witnessing his humiliating fall would make up for all his sneers in the last two days. Now she didn't enjoy her advantage. She didn't care to make someone feel miserable, even if that person was Bernard.

Bernard's sneer was back when he asked, "Still afraid of ghosts?"

She repressed the urge to answer in the same tone and said, "It is spooky down here." She pointed to the dark door in the far wall and asked, "What's in there?"

"A tunnel."

"Where does it lead?"

"Nowhere," Bernard answered. He walked toward the door. "I'll show you."

Bernard picked up a camping lantern that he had hidden in a corner and led the way through the darkened doorway. Twyla followed him and found herself in a hallway running parallel to the room. To the left this hallway dipped down and disappeared in darkness. To the right it ran only about ten feet and ended at a brick wall.

"Watch your step," Bernard warned. "This groove down the middle was for the cable cars that worked the tunnel, probably to carry supplies and ammunition up from the road."

"This leads to the road?" Twyla asked.

Bernard nodded, pointing to the dark shadows. "It ends where we now park the car, though that entrance was sealed up long ago."

Twyla flashed her light in the other direction, toward the brick wall, and stepped closer to investigate a small opening caused by crumbling mortar that had once held the bricks in place.

"What's behind this wall, I wonder?" she said.

"More tunnels. Probably leading all the way to the other tower."

"That far?" she said, bending over to peer through the hole.

"I removed those bricks when we first started working on the remodeling. My mother and father cleaned out the room you found me in and had planned to grow mushrooms there. We may still do it someday."

Twyla hardly heard what Bernard was saying. Her attention was fixed on the hole in the wall. The hole was so small she could barely see through it with the aid of her flashlight. But she managed to view the tunnel on the other side, and saw that it was strewn with loose stones and other debris. Cobwebs seemed to cover everything. She could feel air blowing against her face when she leaned close. And there was a faint odor of garlic from the other side. She mentioned the smell to Bernard.

"Farmers used some of the bunkers for storage at one time. At least that's what I read once," he said.

Twyla took one last sniff then turned and started working her way down the tunnel in the other direction.

"I'm going to bed," Bernard announced. "You can explore if you want, but I'm tired."

Twyla had no desire to explore alone. She, too, headed back to the large room and the stairway. Gitano rushed up the stairs before them and was out of sight by the time they reached the steel door. Bernard turned off the light below at the switch near the door and waited for Twyla to return to her room. He closed the door and threw the bolt, locking it securely.

Twyla stopped at her door to say good night, but Bernard walked past her without a glance and disappeared up the stairs.

She switched off her flashlight, closed her door, and returned to bed. Her book lay face down on the bedside table, where she had abandoned it earlier. She had forgotten all about the absorbing story she had been reading. Her mind was full of her discovery of Bernard on the skateboard and of the disturbing glimpse of unknown stretches of tunnels below.

Bernard had seemed uninterested in what lay on the

other side of that brick wall, though she knew he must have been interested once — he had cared enough to poke a hole in the wall to see what lay on the other side. It must have been at least two years ago, she thought, because she knew his father had died at about that time.

She settled herself in bed, pulling the covers up to her chin, and waited for sleep to come. It took a long time, because she kept remembering the feeling of air on her face through the hole in the wall. She knew that meant there was another opening to the countryside hidden in the forbidden areas of the bunker. She wondered where that opening might be.

The odor of garlic also puzzled her. Bernard had had an answer to that, too. Farmers had stored their produce in the bunker, he said. But that must have been many years ago. Would the smell linger in a place for so long?

10

A Rabbit Shows the Way

Twyla awoke with the sun streaming into the room. It promised another beautiful day. She stretched lazily, like a cat, and thought of the two resolutions she had made last night before falling asleep. The first was that she was going to spend a part of each day searching for another entrance to the bunker. She felt sure there was one. She would honor her promise to Madame Lambert and not poke around in the rock pile on top of the hill, but there had been no restrictions on exploring elsewhere. This she intended to do.

Her second resolution would be harder to keep. She resolved to be friendlier to Bernard, to try to understand him better. She had made this decision because of something she had seen in his eyes last night. She couldn't explain it, but she recognized the feeling it gave her. His eyes had, for a moment, appeared like those of a hurt animal, fearful yet defensive.

She knew he had become ill not long after he had lost his father. He may have been isolated from his friends at the same time he was suffering deeply from his father's death. Twyla remembered the Indian proverb "You should not judge another person until you have walked in his moccasins." In her imagination she walked in those moccasins, and she concluded that it was not a pleasant experience.

Of course, she thought, if it had been her father who had died, she would want to keep active and do things with her friends to keep her mind off her troubles. If she couldn't go out, she would invite friends in — anything to keep herself occupied and to recover from her inner pain. At least she thought she would act this way. But here she was judging again.

Twyla jumped out of bed and dressed, not wanting to waste a single moment of a day when the sun was shining.

Nicholas and Bernard were eating breakfast when she entered the kitchen. Nicholas blurted out that his skateboard had been returned.

"Bernard found it," he said. "And we're going to skateboard in a cement room down below. Bernard is going to take me down there as soon as we finish eating."

Bernard avoided looking at Twyla.

"That's great, Nicky," she said.

"Why don't you come, too?" Nicholas continued. "Bernard says it's a great place for skating — all smooth cement, as big as a ballroom."

"No thanks, Nicky," Twyla said. "I think I'll go out and get some sun."

Bernard seemed relieved. He, no doubt, did not want to repeat last night's humiliating fall. Well, she thought, I'll give him a few days to practice before I watch him skateboard. She knew from experience that it took time to develop your balance and confidence in the sport. Nicholas could teach him a lot. He had been the best sidewalk surfer in his class at school.

When the boys had gone she was joined by her mother. Twyla could see Madame Lambert standing on the deck before an easel, painting. Gitano was stretched out in the sun at her feet.

Twyla's mother was wearing shorts and her nose was covered with a white cream to keep it from burning. She said, "Won't you join me in the sun when you're through eating? It's a glorious day."

"Mmm, I know," said Twyla, her mouth full of her new-found favorite food, croissants. "I may come out later, but I thought I'd take a little hike around the hill first. Did Marie come today?"

"No. Her father delivered the groceries early, before I was up. Cécile has a message for you from Marie."

"Oh?"

"She will tell you about it. I guess you and Marie are friends now. I'm glad. I was a little worried that you might get bored with only the boys for company." Mrs. Jones suddenly looked serious. "I notice that you and Bernard don't seem very friendly toward each other."

"Is it that obvious?" Twyla asked.

Her mother nodded. "I'm afraid so. Cécile noticed it, too, and apologized for her son. He has not had an easy time these last two years."

"I know, Mother. And I've decided to overlook some of Bernard's manners and try to be more understanding."

Her mother smiled and said, "I knew you would. But I'm glad to hear you say it."

When Twyla finished breakfast she cleaned off the table and helped her mother wash the dishes. Then they joined Madame Lambert on the deck to hear the message from Marie.

Madame Lambert continued working on her painting as she talked. The scene on the canvas didn't quite match the view from the deck. But Twyla could praise Madame Lambert's highly original selection of colors.

Twyla said, "It's very nice."

"You don't have to humor me, Twyla," Madame Lambert answered. "I know it's not very good. My art teacher in Paris told me I should give it up. 'Take up petit point,' he said. But I love to work with these new paints. They are so colorful and it is so satisfying to move the paint from the tube to the palette and then to the canvas. It is very good therapy for me."

Mrs. Jones laughed at her friend's frank assessment of her own work. Twyla laughed, too, because she thought

Bernard's mother was one of the most charming and down-to-earth persons she had ever met. She couldn't imagine how her son could be so different.

Madame Lambert smiled mischievously at them and continued to move the paint as she spoke.

"Marie has made a very interesting proposal, I think," she said. "Her father must drive to Épernay on business this afternoon. Marie will go with him as far as Bar-le-Duc, to visit her cousin there. She wants to know if you would like to go with her."

Twyla clasped her hands together and looked at her mother. "May I, Mother?"

"If you want to, of course."

Madame Lambert continued, "It will be an overnight trip, as her father will not be returning until tomorrow. But this is what your mother and I have planned."

She laid the palette and brush down beside her and looked up at Twyla, her eyes sparkling.

"Your mother wants to visit the Verdun battlefields and cemetery and we thought, since you will be almost there, that we would drive to Bar-le-Duc early tomorrow, pick up you and Marie, and continue to Verdun. We can see the sights, have lunch, and then drive back home. What do you think?"

It did not seem to Twyla that a visit to old battlefields would be interesting, but the idea of going with Marie and staying overnight with a different French family appealed to her.

"It sounds like fun," she answered.

"Good," said Madame Lambert. "Then it is settled.

Oh, by the way, Marie mentioned that Madame Courbet goes to Bar-le-Duc occasionally. Monsieur Beury repeated that twice to me. He said Marie made him promise to tell you about Madame Courbet's visits there and that you would know what she meant."

Both women looked at Twyla expectantly, as though they had wondered about the significance of the statement and now waited for an explanation. Twyla felt her heartbeat quicken but she did not say anything.

"Well," said Mrs. Jones. "Do you know why she wanted you to know that?"

"Madame Courbet had a sister who died and is buried there," Twyla said.

Mrs. Jones appeared to be disappointed. Then she and Madame Lambert exchanged looks and shrugged.

Madame Lambert said, "We thought it might be something more exciting."

She returned to her painting and Mrs. Jones stretched out on a chaise longue to enjoy some sunshine. Twyla left them chattering like schoolgirls. They never seemed to run out of things to say to each other. What a joy it must be to have good friends whose friendship never changes, she thought, as she went off to fulfill her first resolution.

Marie and her father would be picking Twyla up after lunch, so this morning she was free to search the area. She started her search on top of the hill, to get her bearings. Bernard had left the ladder against the wall in the yard and she scrambled up and climbed through the vine on top and out onto the flat meadow. It took her a half-hour to pace off the area as she tried to visualize the bunker below. She used the tower of the Lamberts' home as a starting point and walked in a straight line toward the trees. Behind the trees was the ruined tower.

On her left was the drop-off to the valley below. That was the side facing Germany. All the gun emplacements were pointed in that direction. To the right the hill dropped off gently for a way, then there was an escarpment and a thick growth of brush, which made it impossible for her to go farther or even to see the road below. She knew the road was there, however, because she had walked there yesterday.

She did make a new discovery. At intervals, near the escarpment, were ventilation shafts. Twyla discovered the first one by tripping over it. It was partially hidden by long grass and it was plugged up with debris. She found six more just like the first, and one that was not plugged up.

Twyla knelt beside the open shaft and peered down the pipe. Her heart skipped when she felt the telltale draft of air against her face, and again there was the faint odor of garlic she had noticed the night before in the tunnel.

This was all the evidence she needed to know that there was an opening below to another part of the bunker. Excited by her discovery, Twyla went back to the ladder, climbed down, and headed for the road.

She walked up the road in the same direction she had taken the day before, all the way to the end, where the road ran into the hill. She looked up at the vertical cliff to where she could see the tops of the tall trees. That, she decided, was where the ruined tower stood. There was no way to reach the top here. The cliff was too steep to climb and the hillside below the road was also too steep, and the growth of bushes too wild.

Slowly Twyla retraced her steps down the road, keeping her eyes on the right side, looking for some sign of a path or an old road. It was clear to her that if there was another entrance to the bunker along this road, it hadn't been used for many years, probably not since the 1940s, when the bunker had been abandoned.

She had decided that her search was hopeless when a familiar sight confronted her. It was her little rabbit friend of the day before, or at least one very much like him. He stood in her path staring at her for a few seconds before scampering off to the right side of the road. The creature then disappeared by following the same bramble-bush route he had used earlier.

Twyla ran after him. The broken twigs underfoot told her this was the same place she had walked yesterday. Her supposition proved correct a few seconds later when she reached the cement wall again. The rabbit was nowhere in sight. She stopped and listened for any rustle of leaves that would betray the rabbit's movement. There was no sound except for the squawk of a bird scolding her from its perch in the tree above her head. The squawk was answered by a chorus of birds farther away.

Twyla felt as if she were an interloper in this wild

place. The birds and rabbits had had the area to themselves for so long that any intrusion by a human being alarmed them.

Yesterday she had followed the wall to the right until it disappeared. Today Twyla decided to explore the left side of the wall. She slowly picked her way over rocks and through dried branches for about ten feet before she found what she had been looking for.

She was standing in a small clearing with pavement beneath her feet. The pavement was covered by a thick layer of leaves and dried grass. This must be a branch of the road leading to another tunnel.

The cement wall was covered here by a thick growth of vines. The green vines spilled down the steep hillside and over part of the clearing like a waterfall; tough twisted fingers of wood curled out where the leaves had dried or fallen off. It resembled the vine above the Lamberts' side yard that had been tamed and neatly clipped back. This one, however, had grown wild long ago.

Twyla picked up a stick at her feet and poked through the vine as she walked the width of the pavement area. She hit cement on the first three thrusts of the stick but on the fourth thrust the stick disappeared, her hand was suddenly swallowed up by the vine, and a sharp thorn cut into the soft flesh near the base of her thumb.

She dropped the stick and heard it fall on the other side of the vine. The sound of its fall echoed back to her. There must be an open space behind the vine. Twyla was so excited that she immediately forgot about her throbbing hand.

One tangle of vine seemed to hang more loosely than the rest. She pushed on it, then swept it aside. It opened like a drapery, exposing the entrance to a tunnel.

Twyla stepped inside, then let the vine fall back in place. She was now in a space about ten feet wide near the opening, which narrowed farther back and became a tunnel similar to the one Bernard had shown her the night before. There was a groove running along the center of the floor. It seemed to angle gently upward. Twyla wondered if it joined the bricked-up tunnel farther ahead.

She stepped into this hidden tunnel and traveled a short distance before it became too dark to see anything. If only she had remembered to take the flashlight! But she had not expected to find the entrance so quickly.

Twyla was startled by the sound of rustling leaves. She turned to face the vine-shrouded entrance. The loose vines swung gently, as though pushed by the wind, but there was no wind today. It must have been the rabbit, she thought. Her shy little friend who had shown her the way to this secret place had probably made a fast escape.

Twyla approached the entrance again and looked around her. The sun filtered through the leafy vines, making a soft, spotty pattern on the floor and walls inside. The area was bathed in aquamarine light. She felt as if she were in a cool, damp cave behind a waterfall, except that this waterfall made no sound. The quietness of the place gave it an unreal quality. She sniffed the pungent air and felt a glow of satisfaction.

The stillness was broken by a voice somewhere outside, far away, calling her name.

"Twyla!"

It was Nicholas's voice, high and clear. His call upset her. She didn't want to be found here. She wanted to savor her new discovery, her secret, for a while, not sharing it with anyone yet, not even her brother. And she certainly didn't want to share it with Bernard.

She pushed the vines aside and stepped out into the sunshine.

"Twyla!" Nicholas called again. This time his voice was closer, coming from the road beyond the trees, not far from the tunnel entrance.

Twyla hurried away from the tunnel, through the trees, and stepped carefully through a weed-infested ditch that ran beside the road. Once on the road she stopped to get her bearings. She wanted to pick out a landmark that would help her find the tunnel again when she returned.

Across the way lay the pile of logs she had noticed the first time she had walked up this road. They would be her beacon. When she turned back to look toward the hill she was pleased to see that the trees and thick bushes completely hid the cliff and cave entrance. Her secret would be safe for a while.

At that moment Nicholas appeared around a bend in the road.

"Where've you been?" he asked. "Mom sent me to look for you. Marie is here already and you have to come home. We're going to have lunch and then you've gotta leave."

Twyla returned reluctantly to the reality of the moment. She still had to pack for the overnight trip to Bar-le-Duc. She ran to meet her brother and hugged him in greeting.

Nicholas made a face and asked, "What's that for?"

"Just for being you, and my brother," Twyla said. "It's such a glorious day."

Nicholas stepped out of her way and ran ahead of her down the road toward the Lamberts' bunker home. "You're nuts!" he yelled over his shoulder.

Twyla laughed and followed, her spirits soaring.

11

Watery Highways

Twyla knew the drive to Bar-le-Duc would be pleasant with Marie for company. They rode through gently rolling hills and picturesque French villages. She was excited about meeting another French family. Bernard and his mother were French, of course, but Twyla didn't consider them a typical French family. Madame Lambert had adopted many American ways while living in California. Her son had been educated in England. And they lived very comfortably, with an apartment in Paris and the bunker on the Maginot Line.

Twyla suspected Marie's family was more like the majority of French people. Marie spoke about her aunt and uncle as they drove. She had been named for her aunt,

Marie Colline, her father's sister. Of the three Colline children, only one, a seventeen-year-old son, still lived at home. Marie told Twyla that her uncle was a lock keeper.

Twyla imagined a little shop filled with locks and keys on a bustling street in town. This is why she was so surprised when they arrived at the Collines' home.

The last stretch of road followed the Canal de la Marne au Rhin. Marie told Twyla the canal stretched from the Marne River near Paris all the way to the Rhine at Strasbourg. It was only one of many canals criss-crossing France. The canals were hundreds of years old and busy with barges carrying produce, coal, and other goods to cities all over Europe.

"There is Bar-le-Duc," Marie announced.

Twyla looked off to the left and saw the town in the distance. There were some modern buildings on the out-skirts, which contrasted with the old slate roofs of an earlier period. Above them all, on top of the hill over-looking the valley and hillsides, she saw the old town, with its ancient church and clock tower.

Monsieur Beury turned off the road, crossed a bridge, and pulled up into the courtyard of a two-story stone house built alongside the canal.

"Here we are," said Marie.

Twyla looked at the house, the yard, and the struc-tures built over the canal.

"Your uncle is a *canal-lock* keeper!" she said.

"But I told you that," said Marie.

"Yes, I know," said Twyla. "But I thought you meant

locks. You know . . ." She twisted her hand, making the motion of turning a key and snapping a lock closed.

Marie laughed.

The girls got out of the car and Twyla ran to the canal lock, where a bulky barge was preparing to pass through. A young man with black curly hair and lively eyes worked on the lock wall, fastening a rope to a bollard on the topside. He waved to Marie as the two girls walked toward him. Marie introduced Twyla to her cousin Jean.

Jean spoke in French to Marie and she responded by running to the sluice gate and cranking a wheel. Water poured through the opening gate and the barge rose with the rising water until it was level with the bank. It was the first time Twyla had seen how a lock worked and she was fascinated.

The barge filled every square inch of the lock. At the wheel was a middle-aged woman, who had one hand on the throttle and the other resting lightly on the wheel. She appeared to be completely at ease operating the large craft. A black dog stood on the roof of the storage area in front of her. He stared at Twyla and wagged his tail.

Behind the woman the door to the cabin was open. Twyla caught a tantalizing glimpse of the inside of this little house on a barge. She saw the flowered curtains on the windows and a table and chairs. A small girl sat at the table, munching on a crust of bread and watching her mother through the door.

When the water inside the lock was level with the

canal ahead, Marie's cousin ran to another position and cranked a lever that opened the lock gate. The barge passed through. A horn tooted and the woman waved at them and shouted, *"Au revoir!"*

When the excitement was over Marie joined Twyla on the bank and said, "Come. I will introduce you to my aunt and uncle."

Jean spoke again to Marie in French, and Marie translated for Twyla.

"He says they are not home now. They had to go into town on an errand. But they will be home soon."

"You mean they left Jean here all alone to manage the lock?" Twyla gasped.

"Of course. Whoever is home minds the lock. My aunt, and even I, when I am visiting."

Monsieur Beury was just leaving the house as they approached. He told Marie he couldn't wait for his sister but had to go on to Épernay. He kissed his daughter good-by, shook Twyla's hand, and was gone.

Twyla surveyed the setting of the Collines' home. Behind the house was a hill covered with lush green bushes and tall trees, which shielded the property from cold north winds in the winter. There was a small kitchen garden on the west side of the house, neatly kept and full of tomato vines, cabbages, carrots, and some vegetables that Twyla did not recognize.

The front of the house faced the canal and the lock. Graceful poplars grew on both sides of the canal for as far as she could see toward the town of Bar-le-Duc. The road that followed the canal did not have much traffic. There was a busier highway farther away, which carried most of the traffic into town.

The lock remained open, waiting for canal users. Twyla wished she could stay here for a while and work the lock. But right now she was eager to see more of the nearby town.

It was five o'clock. Twyla's mother and Madame Lambert and the boys would be driving by for them the next morning around nine or ten. That didn't leave many daylight hours for Marie to show Twyla the sights. But there was really only one part of town that Twyla was interested in seeing — the cemetery.

"Is it far from here?" she asked Marie.

"Only a short walk, less than a kilometer. It is on the outskirts of town. Do you want to go there now?"

Twyla nodded. "If we have time."

"I have never been inside, myself. There is no one famous buried there. And no one that I know, except for Madame Courbet's sister and brother-in-law. And, of course, I really don't know them. Wouldn't you rather see something else of the town?"

"I have a theory," Twyla said. "I want to see the graves of Madame Courbet's sister and brother-in-law myself."

"What is your theory?" Marie asked.

"I'll tell you when I have proof," said Twyla.

Marie found Jean hard at work behind the house, chopping wood to add to the wood pile. He told Marie he had to finish the job before his parents returned or he wouldn't be able to go into town that night.

"He has a date," Marie told Twyla.

Jean winked at them and asked if they wanted something.

"Only to tell you that we're walking to the cemetery and will be back in an hour," Marie told him in French.

"*Le cimetière?*" he asked.

Marie shrugged. Jean imitated her gesture and they both looked at Twyla, who realized they must think she was crazy.

"O.K." he said. It was his one word of English.

Twyla and Marie set off toward town, following the canal. It was a lovely walk under the poplars. They passed a yacht that was chugging lazily toward the lock.

"Maybe we should have stayed to help Jean," said Marie. "He does want to go to town and will be angry if he doesn't finish the wood."

"We can help him with the wood when we get back if he hasn't finished," said Twyla.

"Do you chop wood?" Marie asked.

Twyla shook her head. "But I could learn."

"I would rather help with the lock," said Marie.

Twyla agreed. Then she told Marie about her discovery of the secret entrance to the tunnels that morning.

Marie seemed surprised. "You found it all by yourself?" she asked.

"Yes. I didn't say anything before, because I didn't want anyone to know," said Twyla. "I want to investigate it before the boys do. If I told them about it earlier they would be exploring it right now while I was here in Bar-le-

Duc. You can explore it with me, if you want to. I would rather have your company than go alone."

"You are not afraid?" Marie asked.

"No. Of course I wouldn't go in if it seemed unsafe. We promised Madame Lambert we wouldn't climb around the ruined tower."

"Ruined tower?"

"I forgot. You haven't heard about that yet," said Twyla. So she told Marie about the maiden flight of the *Nicholas J.* and the discovery of the dynamited tower on top of the hill. At this point they arrived at the gates of the cemetery and both girls forgot about the bunker and concentrated on searching for the graves of Madame Courbet's sister and brother-in-law.

They found the plot of ground they were looking for after a twenty-minute search. The grave was small, near the caretaker's cabin. The headstone was a simple slab of marble with a Cross of Lorraine carved above the name "Theresa LaVesque," and the date of her birth and death were under the name. Beneath, in French, were the words "Courage and Valor."

Marie read the words aloud with reverence. Twyla was overcome with sadness now that she stood before the remains of a woman who had died so young and had done so much for her war-torn country.

"But where is the grave of Charles LaVesque?" she asked.

Marie said, "It should be next to that of his wife. It is customary."

They searched the gravestones on both sides but

found only names they did not know. There was no other grave marked LaVesque, or even Courbet. And none had a date of death that corresponded to that of Theresa LaVesque.

"It's what I thought," said Twyla at last. "My theory is correct. I know it is."

12

The Missing Grave

"But how could you know or even guess that Charles LaVesque was not buried next to his wife?" Marie asked.

The girls were on their way back to the lock, following the canal again. The setting sun glowed a burnt orange in the sky behind them and made their shadows long on the path ahead. The water of the canal reflected the reddish glow and the trees, stirred by a breeze, swayed above their heads.

"Because he isn't dead," said Twyla. "Charles La-Vesque is the man we met on the road in the rain. He is the man we saw leave Madame Courbet's shop."

Marie looked at Twyla. "How could you know such a thing?"

"Elementary, my dear Marie," Twyla answered, in her best Holmesian manner. "Madame Courbet's denying any acquaintance with the man tipped me off. It puzzled me that she would not admit having seen him when we saw him leaving her shop. Why would anyone refute something so obvious? I asked myself. It was her denial that made me so curious about the case. If she had said she didn't know him I would have forgotten about it. Then Nicholas could have kept the medal and everything would have been fine."

Twyla stopped to tie a shoelace. She put her foot up on a bollard next to the canal's edge. There were several of these posts spaced along the canal for boats to be secured to when they anchored for the night. Marie took a seat on another one nearby.

"Then the day we ran into Madame Courbet in church I noticed that she lit only one candle," Twyla continued. "If she were saying a prayer for her dead sister, don't you think she would light a candle also for her sister's husband if he were dead?"

Marie studied Twyla from her perch on the bollard. "What makes you so curious, Twyla?" she asked. "I wouldn't have been. I knew about Madame Courbet's sister, but I never cared to hear more about the story. Since you have been here I have become aware of so many things in my own town and country that never interested me before. You stirred up my interest in the tunnels at the bunker. I have known about those bunkers all my life but I have never before cared to explore them."

They continued on their walk. The lock was in sight

now. There was a car in the courtyard near the front door, which meant the Collines must have returned from town.

"I think I'm interested because it is all new to me," said Twyla. "Sometimes only an outsider is able to show you something you have taken for granted."

"I think I can understand your interest in the tunnels. But why do you care so much about Madame Courbet's family?" Marie asked.

"I guess the mystery of it intrigues me. Coming upon the man as we did in the rain — it was like a scene from a mystery story."

"I have not read many mysteries," said Marie. "But now your mystery is over, is it not?"

"No, Marie. That's the delicious thing about it. It is not solved at all. It is more mysterious than ever."

Marie looked doubtful.

"Don't you see?" Twyla continued. "We don't know anything at all yet, except that Charles LaVesque is not dead and buried next to his wife. If I am right and the stranger in the rain is LaVesque, then there are still many unanswered questions. For example, why did Madame Courbet want it known that he had died with her sister? And why is he still visiting her? Why was she so alarmed that we had seen him and asked her about him? We know that he was involved in secret work during the war, and that raises all sorts of possibilities. There are many parts to Madame Courbet's riddle."

They had reached the courtyard and stopped before going into the house.

"I don't think I like your mysteries, Twyla," said

Marie. "There is no hope of solving them, and that leaves me with an unsettled feeling."

"But we must solve them," said Twyla. "Surely someone must know more about Theresa and her work in the Underground during the war."

Marie's interest perked up again. "Maybe so. If we could find someone we could ask . . ." she stopped. "Oh, but we couldn't ask such questions of a stranger."

"You're right, of course," said Twyla.

The girls sat on a bench near the door.

Finally Marie said, "Perhaps my aunt and uncle would know. My uncle grew up in Bar-le-Duc, and since Theresa is buried here, she must have died nearby. During the war there would have been no time to move the body to her own town for burial. She would be buried close to where she was killed, don't you think?"

Twyla agreed.

They entered the house, where they found the Collines in the large country kitchen. Monsieur Colline was as handsome as his son. He smiled at Twyla when they were introduced. Madame Colline was busy at the marble-top table, rolling pastry for dinner. Her eyes sparkled with good humor and she beamed when she heard that Twyla was an American.

"I have not talked to many Americans," Madame Colline said. "Not since the American army left France, in 1966. There was an American army depot near here before that time, and Bar-le-Duc was always full of young Americans. We spoke your language often when they were here. But I'm afraid my English is not as good now, since I no longer have the opportunity to speak it."

Twyla wished she could speak French as well as both the Collines spoke English. She said this to Madame Colline.

"But you have not had the opportunity. This is your first visit to France, *n'est-ce pas?*"

"Yes. But I did study French for a year in school."

Madame Colline waved her hands in the air. "*Pouf!* What is one year? We study foreign languages in school, too. But we did not learn to speak English until the Americans came and we had to use the language."

A horn tooted from the direction of the canal. Monsieur Colline left his half-filled cup of coffee on the table and went to work the lock. Twyla would have liked to follow, but Madame Colline had put her and Marie to work making a salad for the evening meal.

"So, where have you girls been this afternoon?" Madame Colline asked.

Marie told her.

"*Le cimetière?* You should have gone into town to see the shops and the living people of Bar-le-Duc. You are too young to concern yourselves with the dead."

Twyla signaled Marie with her eyes that she should ask her aunt about Madame Courbet's sister.

Marie understood and said, "Twyla wanted to see where Theresa LaVesque is buried."

"Theresa LaVesque? She was a friend of yours, Twyla?" Madame Colline asked.

"Oh, no. But I met her sister in St. Germain."

"Madame Courbet," Marie added.

"Ah, oui! I remember now. Madame Courbet often drives here with your papa."

Twyla's next attempt to signal Marie was intercepted by Madame Colline, who asked, "What is it? You wish to ask me a question?"

"We wondered why Theresa's husband was not buried with her," Marie said.

"You want to find his grave, too? Well, I wish I could help but I do not know the family. My husband may know. He knows more about what goes on in town than I do. He goes to the café and the men gossip like old ladies." Madame Colline laughed and threw her hands in the air again, sending a puff of flour flying. "And they say women are the gossips!"

Monsieur Colline entered the kitchen again and settled down to enjoy his coffee. Madame Colline said something to him in French and he listened intently, then turned to Twyla and said, "You are interested to know about Madame Courbet's family?"

Twyla nodded. "But it is an old story. Theresa LaVesque died during the war."

Marie jumped into the conversation. "She and her husband worked in the Underground. They were shot — at least she was shot — by the Nazis as a spy."

In the next few minutes Twyla and Marie told the Collines the whole story. Madame Colline shook her head at last and said, "The poor young lovers! What a sad ending." She wiped a tear from her eyes.

Her husband was also touched by the story. He said, "I have heard about the fate of Theresa LaVesque before, but it has been so many years since the war. I was just a young boy, but I did run errands for the local Maquis."

"The Maquis?" Twyla asked.

"The name they went by — the Underground."

"And you worked with them, too?" Marie asked.

"Only a few times," he said with pride. "They were a brave group. Many were killed. There is a village near here where every man and boy was killed for the bombing of one Nazi train. No one would confess to the attack. The Nazis were desperate to teach all French men and women a lesson. So they shot all men and boys of the village. Then they burned the houses to the ground, leaving the survivors homeless." He shook his head. "In wartime such things happen."

Twyla gasped in horror. "That is barbaric!" she said.

"Ah, but you see, *ma petite Américaine,* during a war men become like animals. That is why we should work to maintain peace always."

Madame Colline had finished rolling her pastry and had set it aside. She blew her nose and then smiled.

"Perhaps it is good to remember such sad stories from time to time, so we won't forget the tragedy of war. But now we will put that aside."

Monsieur Colline said, "If you are interested in finding out what happened to Charles LaVesque, then you should talk with Monsieur Dusseault. He is a very old man who once was the leader of the local Maquis."

"Did he know the LaVesques?" Marie asked.

"If anyone knew them, he did."

"Where does he live?" Twyla asked.

"He lives in Bar-le-Duc. In the old town up on the hill. But you can find him every night at the café in the Hôtel de Metz. He goes there to talk to his old friends. Not many of them are left."

Twyla jumped up and down with delight nearly up-setting the basket of lettuce she had prepared. Then she remembered that they would be leaving in the morning. There would be no opportunity to meet Monsieur Dusseault and ask about the LaVesques.

Her fears ended when Monsieur Colline said, "You can go into town tonight with Jean. He will show you the café and I will give you the password to say to Monsieur Dusseault so he will talk to you." Monsieur Colline winked at them. "He still likes to play the game, like in the old days."

Monsieur Colline described Monsieur Dusseault to them and told them that he usually sat at the corner table by the windows. If it was a warm evening, however, the old man might be sitting at a table outside on the side-walk.

"You will go to him and say 'Bonsoir. The traffic on the canal is very heavy today.' That is my code to him. He will know you have been sent by me and he will re-ceive you."

It sounded exciting to Twyla, like a scene in a spy movie.

"Does Monsieur Dusseault speak English?" she asked.

"Of course," said Monsieur Colline. "He often worked with the English and Americans during the war.

When an Allied pilot was shot down behind German lines, he would hide the man until he could help him get to the English Channel for transportation back to safety."

Twyla waited impatiently until it was time to go into town. The lock closed at 7:30 in the evening. Then the family had their supper, at the kitchen table. First fish was served, followed by the meat dish, which tonight was a delicious kidney pie baked in the pastry Madame Colline had made. The salad came next. They completed the meal with fruit and cheese.

When Madame Colline told Jean he was to take the girls into town with him that night, Twyla could see he didn't enjoy the thought of sharing his date. His mother explained that they were going to the café to meet a friend. Later they could go to the movies and he could pick them up at midnight, when the movie was over.

This plan seemed agreeable to him. He nodded and said "O.K." to Twyla. He would still be able to take his young lady to the dance and not have to waste part of the evening with Twyla and Marie.

13

Secret Agents
of the Maquis

Twyla and Marie helped Madame Colline wash the dishes and then dressed for their night out in Bar-le-Duc. Jean was impatient to go. When the girls finally emerged from the house they found him with a rag in his hand, dusting off the family automobile for the third time. He smiled when they appeared, opened the door to hurry them into the car, then drove off, down the poplar-lined road into town.

It was a five-minute drive to the Rue de la Rochelle, the main promenade in town. The sidewalks were crowded with people strolling in the fine evening air. Jean told them that the weather was not often so mild, and when it was, everyone made the most of it.

He stopped the car at a corner near the Hôtel de

Metz, first pointing out the movie theater up the street where he would pick them up after the show.

Twyla felt her heart beating double time in anticipation of their rendezvous with Monsieur Dusseault. She and Marie walked slowly toward the tables in front of the hotel.

"What if he isn't here tonight?" Marie asked Twyla.

"Don't even think of such a thing," Twyla answered.

Twyla knew her friend was just as excited as she was. She saw that Marie studied every man they passed, looking for the one her uncle had described.

They reached the hotel and took a table near the entrance. Most of the tables were already taken but they could see no one who might be Monsieur Dusseault. Monsieur Colline had said he was an old man, over seventy, with a rather large stomach. He had white hair and a white mustache, and always wore a black beret. There were at least ten men wearing berets at the tables outside, but none fit the rest of the description.

"Maybe he's inside the hotel," said Twyla.

Marie left her seat to peek in the door. When she returned she said, "I don't see him inside, either. We will just have to wait."

They ordered bottles of soda and sipped slowly. Twyla was fascinated by the parade of people and cars that flowed by. Traffic was bumper to bumper on the street. The sound of motors and the beeping of horns were constant. Whole families walked together, with children racing around their parents' legs. Several old men approached. This raised the girls' expectations, but the men walked on.

At last one old man appeared at the café and turned in their direction. He paused, looking for an empty seat. Twyla grabbed Marie's arm and whispered, "That's him. It must be Monsieur Dusseault. He fits the description your uncle gave us exactly."

Marie agreed. "Shall we ask him to join us at our table?" she said.

"Yes. But first you should use the code words. Do you remember them?"

Marie nodded. The man was just a few feet away. She walked up to him and Twyla heard her say *"Bonsoir."* Then she spoke the rest of the code phrase in French. Twyla watched as the man studied Marie with a wary eye. Marie said something else and he looked at Twyla.

She felt herself grow smaller under his direct gaze. His eyes were black and bright, capable of withering a weak soul at a glance. She grabbed her bottle of soda and tried to look nonchalant as he walked toward the table and took a seat. Marie sat next to Twyla and both girls waited for him to speak.

The waiter appeared, and asked for the man's order. He seemed to know Monsieur Dusseault well. The two men exchanged words about family and weather before the waiter left to fill the order. Still Monsieur Dusseault did not speak. He sat back in his chair, folded his hands over his prominent stomach, and stared at the girls.

Twyla was nervous. She gulped and said in a wavery

voice, "The traffic on the canal is very heavy today, Monsieur Dusseault."

The words spoken in English must have stirred something in the old man's memory. His eyebrows moved up and down and he said, very softly, "So, you are American?"

"Yes," she answered.

"It has been many, many years since I have heard those words spoken by an American."

Twyla thought she saw a tear form in one of his eyes. He blinked it away and said, "You have some information for me, Mademoiselle . . . ?"

"Jones. Twyla Jones. And this is Marie Beury."

Monsieur Dusseault looked at Marie and asked, "And where do you come from, Mademoiselle Beury?"

"From St. Germain, *monsieur*. But my aunt and uncle live here. The Collines. My uncle said — "

He didn't let her finish. "Yes. I know them. A good man, your uncle. He was very helpful in our work."

He sat silently. His drink was served, and he seemed to wait for them to make the next move.

Twyla said, "We don't have any information for you, but we thought you might be able to help us."

"What is it you want?"

"We — we want to know where Charles LaVesque is," she answered.

Monsieur Dusseault looked away from her, toward the traffic on the street, but he didn't look as though he saw the cars and the people passing by. He seemed to be gazing beyond them, at another place and time. The muscles in his face twitched, and Twyla was afraid he had forgotten her question.

She waited for him to look back at them. Several minutes passed before he did. When he finally faced them she thought he appeared older. His head drooped and he seemed very sad.

"She volunteered for her last mission," Monsieur Dusseault said. "I told Charles LaVesque that she had done so and that he shouldn't blame himself if she met with misfortune. But he insisted on following her on his bicycle. That was the fatal mistake — the bicycle."

He cleared his throat, took a long sip of his drink, and continued. "Before going on the mission Theresa had said that a woman would not be suspect at that time of day. So she took the explosive under her coat and walked to the ammunition truck. No one stopped her. No one suspected her. She planted the explosive on the truck and walked on. She was far away when it blew up. She was safe. But, as I told you, Charles had followed her. He caught up with her and insisted that she take his bicycle.

"She rode off while he walked back to our headquarters. We later heard that she had been stopped by the Nazis in the next village for questioning. They took the bicycle apart and discovered a radio receiver hidden inside. They knew then that she was a member of the Maquis. They had all the evidence they needed to shoot her on the spot."

Monsieur Dusseault stopped. Twyla was breathless. She was overcome with horror by this account of an actual Maquis mission during the war.

"Charles LaVesque was inconsolable," Monsieur Dusseault continued. "He blamed himself, of course. He was never again the same man. He still was a good, brave Maquis. But the light had gone out of his life. I have not seen him for many years. Theresa is buried here in Bar-le-Duc."

"We know. We visited her grave today," said Twyla.

"She was very brave and very beautiful," he said. "She was too young to die. Charles appeared again after the war and lived in Verdun for a short time. But he was a different man —not like the old Charles. He was a recluse."

Marie looked at Twyla and asked, "What is that?"

"Like a hermit," said Twyla. "A recluse cuts himself off from other people and lives alone."

Monsieur Dusseault nodded. "That was what he had become. A friend in Verdun got him into a hospital for treatment and that seemed to help him for a while. I saw him then — in Verdun, at the home of a friend. But Charles had great problems. And soon after I saw him he disappeared again. I have not seen or heard of him again. That was ten years ago."

"Ten years?" asked Twyla.

"Perhaps he is dead by now," Monsieur Dusseault said.

"No, he is not dead," said Twyla. "We saw him just a few days ago in St. Germain."

The bushy white eyebrows flew up as the old man looked at her. "You have seen him? But you have just asked me if I knew where he is."

"Yes. We saw him but we want to know where he is living. We have something that belongs to him."

Monsieur Dusseault sat forward and asked, "What is it you have?"

"It's a Cross of Lorraine," said Twyla. She described it to him then said, "He dropped it in our car one night when we picked him up in the rain. My brother found it on the floor later, and we want to give it back to him."

Monsieur Dusseault nodded. "That would be the cross that Theresa received for her work with the Maquis. The last time I saw it was the day she was buried. It was around her neck as she lay in the casket." He shook his head again and looked sad. "She was so young and so beautiful."

Again he was lost in his own thoughts. Twyla was almost sorry she had met with him tonight, for this meeting seemed to have opened old wounds. Monsieur Dusseault appeared to have aged these last few minutes.

When he spoke again he had regained some of his original spirit. His eyes were clear and he sat up straight in his chair.

"I am sorry I cannot help you find the man you seek. But I know someone who may be able to help you. He is in Verdun."

"We are going there tomorrow," said Twyla. "We are going to visit the battlefields."

"Then you are in luck. Monsieur Dotti works as a

guide at Douaumont. Do you know where that is?"

Twyla said no. But she was sure Bernard would know.

"Then I will tell you what you must do," he said. "When you get to the Ossuary of Douaumont, you must ask for Monsieur Dotti. And when you find him you must say, 'Jacques sends greetings from Trois Fontaines.'"

Twyla repeated the phrase then reached for a pencil and notebook from her purse to write it down. Monsieur Dusseault stopped her.

"Never write anything down. It is too dangerous. You must remember the code in your head."

He tapped his head and winked. Twyla couldn't tell if he was just joking or if he really believed it was still dangerous to write out a secret code on paper.

Marie asked him, "Do you know why Madame Courbet, his sister-in-law, would deny knowing him?"

"No. I cannot say any more than what I have already told you. You must ask Monsieur Dotti. He will know, if anyone does."

It was clear that Monsieur Dusseault had had enough of the past. He ordered another drink and then he hailed a passing friend. Twyla and Marie said good-by and thanked him. He seemed to have forgotten them already. He waved absently as he began chatting with the new arrival.

14

Mission to Verdun

Twyla and Marie awoke at dawn, both excited at the prospect of their mission to Verdun.

The Colline family was already at work when the girls appeared for breakfast. Madame Colline had food ready for them. Her husband and son were outside at the lock, tending to the early-morning canal traffic. Twyla and Marie ate quickly, then went out to help the men.

The morning air was brisk in spite of a bright sun. The slant of the sun reminded Twyla that school would soon begin. This year she would have unusual memories to sustain her through the winter months. Since coming to Europe she had seen so many new sights. Before, she could not have imagined that she would be opening sluice gates to a lock and casting off lines to barges in the center of France, nor that she would find herself living in an underground bunker. These were her thoughts as she worked alongside Jean, his father, and Marie that morning.

Twyla's mother, Nicholas, and the Lamberts arrived at nine o'clock. They, too, had been up since dawn, in order to get an early start. Twyla hugged her mother and tried to do the same to Nicholas, but he ducked out of reach. Nicholas was in an exuberant mood, full of all the new sights he had seen on the road.

"Bernard showed me where a real dirigible was shot down by the French in 1916," he told Twyla.

He was fascinated by the working of the lock and was thrilled when Monsieur Colline allowed him to open the sluice for a barge.

"Neato!" he cried, as the barge passed through. "Gee, it's fun to be in France. They do so many neat things here."

Twyla tried to tell him that there were probably many little boys like him living in France who never came close to a lock, but he was too busy helping Monsieur Colline to pay attention. Twyla went into the kitchen with her mother and Madame Lambert. Madame Colline had coffee ready and insisted they all have some food before leaving.

An hour later they were on the road, headed for Verdun and a day of exploring the site of the bloodiest battle during World War I. The road they followed was known as the Voie Sacrée, or Sacred Road. Bernard told them this had been the main route for French reinforcements. During the fiercest fighting of 1916 two thousand trucks had passed along this road daily in each direction, carrying men and supplies to the Verdun front.

Bernard's voice droned on and on. Twyla thought he sounded like a dull history textbook. But her thoughts were mainly on the expected meeting with the agent in Verdun, so Bernard's tour-guide routine didn't bother her.

As they neared Verdun there was a sharp change in the terrain. Instead of flat meadows and smooth-topped hills, the ground was pocked with craters. Except for some scattered grass, the area resembled a moonscape. Bernard explained that this was a result of the terrible shelling the whole area had gone through during the years of the First World War when the opposing armies were stalemated here.

"The land will never recover from those years," he said. "There are parts of the Argonne Forest to the west that are still dangerous to go into. In fact it is forbidden. Farmers still dig up bombs with their plows. The remains of soldiers who died sixty years ago and were covered up by more bomb blasts are still being found."

Nicholas sat with his nose pressed to the car window surveying the scene.

"Not long ago," Bernard continued, "some children playing in the woods came upon an old biplane hanging in the trees with a skeleton at the controls."

"Golly!" said Nicholas.

Twyla shuddered. Mrs. Jones said, "I'm glad you are so well informed, Bernard. We should learn a great deal about the wars from you today."

Madame Lambert said, "Bernard is specializing in history in his studies. He is interested particularly in the two world wars."

Twyla had to admit that some of the facts did arouse her interest — like the skeleton pilot of the fallen airplane. Whereas historical facts offered as a mass of dates and statistics meant little to her, she found compelling the more intimate notes of history, such as Theresa's heroism and the ill-fated plane.

Verdun was a town of moderate size and it was busy with traffic. It was a shock to come off the country roads into the commotion in the Verdun streets. Madame Lambert parked the car near the Victory monument and they walked around for an hour before having lunch at a pleasant café near the river.

Twyla and Marie sat next to each other at lunch, trying to exchange their secret thoughts. Both were eager to get to the battlefields at Douaumont for their meeting with Monsieur Dotti.

"Do you remember the code?" Twyla whispered once. Marie nodded.

Nicholas, who sat on the other side of Marie, overheard the question. "What code?" he asked.

"It doesn't concern you," Twyla said to him.

Nicholas was disappointed to be left out of their conversation. Twyla noticed that although he appeared to be engrossed in talk with Bernard, he stopped whenever she spoke to Marie. There was no chance for a private word. Twyla and Marie had to be content with secret looks and smiles, which seemed to increase Nicholas's curiosity. When they left the restaurant and walked back to the car he stuck to them like Scotch tape, never letting them out of earshot.

Outside of Verdun, on the road to Metz, they passed the National Cemetery of Faubourg Pavé, which contains four thousand war dead. Bernard pointed out a monument built to honor André Maginot, the French politician after whom the Maginot Line was named. Madame Lambert drove farther on to a special monument dedicated to the memory of sixteen French patriots shot without trial by the Germans in 1944, during the Second World War. Twyla thought of Theresa LaVesque and wondered if any of the sixteen patriots had been her friends.

The whole area they now drove through was so full of the history of both world wars that Twyla soon found her head was full of facts and dates. By the time they reached the Ossuaire de Douaumont — Ossuary of Douaumont — she was no longer listening. She knew that this was the most impressive of the area's monuments. They were surrounded by nearly half a million dead war heroes. Many of them were American, most of whom were unidentified. She was shocked by the enormous number of battle victims. After listening to more of the tragedy, she decided she had had enough history for one day.

Nicholas's interest hadn't diminished. "French words

are funny," he said. "What does *ossuaire* mean, anyway?"

"The word comes from the Latin," said Bernard. "An ossuary is a depository of the bones of the dead."

The Ossuary of Douaumont was a long building shaped like an inverted trench and rounded on top. It reminded Twyla of a very large Quonset hut, but unlike a Quonset hut, this was built of stone. A tower rose from the center of the structure. Bernard told them the tower had been paid for by the American people. Inside was a Catholic chapel, and throughout the building were buried the remains of many unidentified war dead.

"We can climb up the tower if you want to," Bernard said. "From the top we will get the best view of the battlefields and monuments."

The mothers declined the strenuous climb. Nicholas was ready to climb anything as long as Bernard led the way. Twyla and Marie grasped this opportunity to break away from the group and search out Monsieur Dotti. As soon as the boys were gone, and Mrs. Jones and Madame Lambert had wandered away to read the plaques honoring the dead, the girls walked to the front of the building to look for a tour guide.

They were approached by one almost immediately. He was a young man and eager to show them the points of interest. He offered them a special low price. The young guide was so charming that Twyla was tempted to accept his offer, but Marie told him they were looking for Monsieur Dotti, a special friend.

"Do you know him?" she asked.

"*Oui*. I know him," said the young man. He appeared unhappy to have lost the opportunity of guiding two attractive tourists. "Monsieur Dotti has taken another group around to the Trench of Bayonets. Do you know where that is?"

They told him they did not.

"It is just behind this place," he told them. "It is a monument erected above the bodies of French soldiers buried while fighting. Through the windows you can see the bayonets sticking up out of the soil." At the moment no other tourists waited for his services, so he smiled and said, "I will take you there. For you there will be no charge."

Twyla and Marie agreed and followed him to the trench. On the way he told them of the nine villages in the area that had been wiped out. He mentioned again the number of men who had died here. After a while he stopped talking. He had no way of knowing they had already heard most of what he said from Bernard.

Near the Trench of Bayonets a man approached them on the path. He was short and wiry, dressed all in black, with a black beret on his bald head.

"Here is Monsieur Dotti now," said their young guide. To the old man he said, "I have brought you two young friends."

The young tour guide bid them farewell and departed.

Twyla and Marie introduced themselves to Monsieur Dotti. Then Marie said in English, "Jacques sends greetings from Trois Fontaines."

Monsieur Dotti gave them a questioning look and

asked, "You wish to see the American Cemetery? I had thought to take a quick rest but I suppose — "

Marie repeated, "Jacques sends his greetings from Trois Fontaines."

"From Trois Fontaines, you say?" said Monsieur Dotti.

He seemed puzzled and Twyla feared they had been misled by Monsieur Dusseault. Just because he was still living in the days of the Maquis of World War II didn't mean everyone else remembered. She was about to tell Marie they had better join the others of their party when a light came into Monsieur Dotti's eyes.

He smiled and said, "But of course. Jacques. *Pardon, mesdemoiselles,* but it has been a long time since I have had word from Jacques in Trois Fontaines. Come. You will walk with me to Douaumont and tell me what it is you wish."

Marie began. "We are looking for Charles La-Vesque."

Monsieur Dotti's pace slowed but he continued walking, his eyes on the hills above Verdun, as Marie spoke.

"We have the Cross of Lorraine that belonged to Theresa LaVesque. Twyla's brother found it in the Jones's car. We think Charles LaVesque dropped it there after an accident involving his bicycle and the car."

"You are friends with Charles LaVesque, *mademoiselle?*" he asked Twyla.

"Not really," she answered. Then she explained how they had met him on the rainy road, and how she had seen him again in St. Germain, but that Madame Courbet had refused to acknowledge his visit to her shop.

"We have been trying to find him ever since," she added.

They had reached the front steps of the Douaumont monument. Twyla looked around quickly and could see no sign of the boys or her mother and Madame Lambert. She was relieved, since she wasn't prepared to explain to them about her search for LaVesque.

Marie said, "We think he should have the medal back. It must mean a great deal to him."

Monsieur Dotti nodded. His right hand rubbed his chin. He took his time before speaking, as though he wanted to say the right words.

Finally, he said, "Madame Courbet is honoring La-Vesque's wishes when she does not speak of him. He has not been well for the many years since Theresa was executed. He believes he is responsible for her death, you understand?"

Twyla nodded. "But he wasn't responsible, was he?"

"No. Circumstances were against them. Still, no one could convince him of his innocence, so he ran away and hid until the war was over. As you may know, he is an American."

Twyla and Marie nodded.

"He believes he is a fugitive from American law, because he did not report back to the army after his last mission. For this reason he has told Madame Courbet that his whereabouts must never be known. Madame Courbet is desperate to protect him, so she tells everyone that he died with Theresa."

"Is he in trouble with the Americans?" Twyla asked.

"No. Long ago he was exonerated from any charges. He was in hospital then for treatment. He does not remember everything too clearly," Monsieur Dotti said.

"Doesn't Madame Courbet know that?" Marie asked. "And couldn't she make him believe that he no longer has to hide?"

Monsieur Dotti shook his head and lifted his sad brown eyes to her face. "He is a very sick man. I have told him that for what he has done *he* deserves a medal. But he lives in his own imaginary world now. His twisted mind creates illusions that he believes are real. Perhaps Madame Courbet believes them to be true. I do not know. I never see her — not since her sister was buried in Bar-le-Duc, and that is many years ago."

He sat down on the steps of Douaumont and the girls sat beside him.

"We can tell her," Twyla said at last. "We must tell her all you have told us. Then if she knows where he is she can reveal his secret place and we can return the cross to him."

Marie seemed skeptical. Twyla could understand her feelings. She herself had no desire for another interview with Madame Courbet, but it seemed necessary.

Monsieur Dotti said, "You could do that. But it may be too late."

"Too late?" Twyla questioned.

"I saw Charles LaVesque just last month. He told me he was preparing to die and he had come to say good-by. I have not heard from him since. I fear he may have crawled off into a hidden corner just as a dog does when he knows that he is ill."

"Oh, no!" Marie cried.

"But we saw him just a few days ago," Twyla said.

"He was perhaps saying good-by to Madame Courbet at the time you saw him," Monsieur Dotti said. "I wish you luck, my dear friends. It is well that you are trying to find him to return the Cross of Lorraine. If he were able, I am sure Charles LaVesque would thank you."

He stood and they followed. Then he grabbed Twyla by her shoulders and kissed her on both cheeks. He did the same to Marie. Then he said, "*Vive la France! Vive l'Amérique!* And long live the spirit of the Maquis!"

He turned and left them there at the bottom of the steps staring after him as he walked with dignity up the stairs and disappeared inside the Ossuary of Douaumont.

Within seconds, Nicholas ran up to them and asked, "Who was that man and why did he kiss you?"

Twyla jumped at the sound of his voice and turned to face her little brother. "He was a tour guide," she said.

"But he kissed you!" Nicholas cried. "Does Mom know you are letting strange men kiss you?"

"Nicholas!" Twyla said, exasperated.

But Nicholas did not wait for an explanation. "Keep your old secrets. See if I care," he said. "We have a secret, too, and I was going to tell you about it, even though Bernard told me not to. But now I won't!"

He turned and ran up the steps to meet his mother, who with Madame Lambert had just appeared at the entrance to Douaumont.

Twyla turned to Marie and said, "He will spoil everything."

They waited for the others at the foot of the steps. Twyla surveyed the thousands of graves that stretched in rows before her. She knew that the burials represented terrible misery for so many families. It was almost too great a tragedy for her to comprehend. Closer to her heart was the tragedy of one death — that of Theresa LaVesque, buried in a small grave in an obscure cemetery near Bar-le-Duc. Twyla understood the heartache Theresa's death had caused Charles LaVesque and Madame Courbet.

She could do little about the misery the endless rows of graves had caused, but perhaps she could do something about the LaVesque tragedy. She wasn't sure how, but she knew she *must* do something.

15

A Visit with Madame Courbet

It was a long drive back to the Lamberts' bunker home. They made two stops, once near Metz to view the remains of a Roman aqueduct, and once for dinner in the mountain town of Saverne. Twyla dozed in the back seat. Bernard finally had nothing more to say about the history of the Alsace-Lorraine region of France. Nicholas alternately stared at his sister and then whispered to Bernard — probably about the secret he had mentioned earlier.

Mrs. Jones shared the driving with Madame Lambert. She started to speak to Twyla a few times during the trip home but hesitated each time. Twyla wondered what Nicholas had told her. She was sure she would find out soon.

They first took Marie home to St. Germain, then drove to the bunker. It was past midnight before Twyla was settled in her bed. She was weary from the day's activities but unable to sleep, because of the excitement of all that had happened, especially meeting with the two former members of the French Underground.

She turned her light off and waited for sleep to come. Minutes later there was a light knock on her door and her mother entered, carrying two cups of hot chocolate on a tray.

"I thought you might still be awake," she said. "Want some?"

Twyla accepted the cup and said, "I'm having trouble relaxing."

Mrs. Jones took a seat near the foot of the bed. "Too much excitement in two short days, I imagine," she said. "You can relax tomorrow. Sleep late. Marie won't be here, because it's Saturday."

Twyla had forgotten what day it was. She realized that she wouldn't see Marie until Monday morning. It would be two days before they could explore the tunnel, she thought.

"Did Nicholas tell you about the tour guide at Douaumont?" Twyla asked.

"He did mention something shocking about you and Marie kissing a strange old man on the steps," her mother said, laughing. "Care to tell me about it?"

Twyla began by telling about her first confrontation with Madame Courbet in the shop, when they asked her about the stranger riding away on a bicycle. The story poured out and Mrs. Jones listened intently without interrupting. Only once did she show her disapproval. This was when Twyla related the incident in the church that had frightened Madame Courbet and caused her to flee.

When Twyla finished her account of their meeting with Monsieur Dotti in Verdun she leaned back on her pillow and sipped her hot chocolate. She felt drained of all energy. By telling her story she had released all the tension that had built up inside her. She was able to relax at last. Twyla yawned and pulled the covers up to her chin.

Mrs. Jones said, "You have been busy, haven't you?"

Twyla nodded sleepily. "We didn't say anything about it before because it was our mystery. Marie and I wanted to solve it by ourselves. But we were going to tell you eventually."

Mrs. Jones smiled. "A mystery isn't so much fun if everyone knows about it."

"I knew you would understand," said Twyla.

"Of course, you will have to apologize to Madame Courbet for frightening her in church."

Twyla nodded.

"And you will have to be diplomatic when you give her Monsieur Dotti's message. She may resent having a stranger such as you delving into her family's troubles."

Twyla agreed and already felt uncomfortable about the eventual meeting with Madame Courbet.

Her mother continued, "Of course, if she had told

you the truth at the beginning — about knowing Charles LaVesque — you would have given her the medal and that would have been the end of it."

"That's what I thought, too," said Twyla. "But when she didn't, well, we had to search out the facts ourselves."

"Would you like me to go with you to explain your strange action to Madame Courbet?" Mrs. Jones asked.

"Oh, yes, Mother," said Twyla, feeling better.

Standing beside Twyla's bed, her mother said, "We will go to her shop as soon as you feel rested. Maybe tomorrow afternoon. Now try to get some sleep."

"I will. Thank you, Mother. I'm very sleepy now."

Her mother left the room. Twyla snuggled down under the fluffy comforter and closed her eyes. It was so quiet in the bunker tonight; so quiet she could hear her heart beating. She listened to it for a while before she realized it wasn't her heart she heard but the rhythmic beat of the bunker itself, as though this old hill had a living heart of its own that pulsed through the walls all around her.

It was not the tinlike tapping she had heard her first night in the bunker. That had been more sporadic and not as muted as this sound. This beating seemed to be all around her and yet far, far away. She was too sleepy to be concerned about it. The sound stopped a short time later and Twyla slept deeply until morning.

When she finally awoke, at ten o'clock, she first checked the view from her room. She was disappointed to see a fine mist of drizzle falling from a lead-colored sky. It was not a good day for outdoor activity. The weather, however, didn't hamper the boys' plans. They disappeared downstairs as soon as they had eaten breakfast. Nicholas had his skateboard under one arm. He and Bernard were eager to pursue the sport in the underground cavern.

Twyla hadn't been invited to join them, but she didn't mind. Instead, she spent two hours reading before the fire in the warm family room upstairs. It took her almost an hour to read one chapter. She gazed into the flames, thinking about Charles LaVesque and Theresa and reliving the last two days in Bar-le-Duc and Verdun.

Bernard and Nicholas appeared at lunchtime, bolted their food, and then returned to their skateboarding. Mrs. Jones joined Twyla by the fire about midafternoon and suggested a drive to St. Germain.

"Cécile needs a few things before Monday and I volunteered our services," she said. "It will be a good opportunity to have our visit with Madame Courbet. That is, if you are in the mood and ready to talk to her."

Twyla put her book aside. "I'll go with you. I'm not concentrating on my reading, anyway."

Mrs. Jones had taken the Cross of Lorraine from Nicholas during the morning. She gave it to Twyla now to keep until they reached St. Germain. They borrowed umbrellas from Madame Lambert, wrapped themselves in raincoats, and were off.

St. Germain was more crowded than it had been on the last market day. It seemed as if every person in town were shopping for weekend supplies. They stopped at the meat market first, then the greengrocer and the pharmacy. They avoided the crowded marketplace in the church square, which was full of activity in spite of the damp weather.

Bread was the last item on their shopping list. Madame Courbet's shop was filled with customers. They waited patiently to place their order with the owner.

"Please hand me the medal, Twyla," Mrs. Jones asked.

Twyla gave it to her mother, who slipped it into the pocket of her raincoat as Madame Courbet turned toward them.

The Frenchwoman seemed to tower over them. It wasn't that she was so tall, Twyla decided. It was the way she stood, so straight and stiff. The severe cut of her black dress, the black hair pulled straight back and up into a knot, all added to the illusion of height.

There was a flicker of recognition in her eyes as she looked at Twyla. Then she said to them, "*Mesdames?*"

Twyla was relieved she hadn't come with Marie for this confrontation. Marie could not measure up to Madame Courbet's stern presence, and Twyla wondered whether her mother could do any better. But she had no reason to be concerned. Her mother spoke adequate French and was a strong-willed person.

Mrs. Jones ordered four loaves of bread and a dozen croissants. Madame Courbet got the order together and helped pack the items into the string shopping bag. Mrs. Jones paid with a large bill and received her change.

As the money was exchanged Twyla's mother slipped

her hand into her pocket and took out the Cross of Lorraine. She laid it on the counter in front of Madame Courbet. Twyla waited for the Frenchwoman's reaction.

Madame Courbet stood ramrod-straight looking down at the cross. It seemed an eternity before she spoke, and when she did Twyla was sure the woman's shoulders had slumped a little.

"Where did you get this?" she asked finally, her voice husky with emotion.

"We found it in our car," Mrs. Jones said. "A man we picked up on the road must have dropped it there. We have reason to believe you may know the man and can get it back to him."

They spoke in French. Twyla could understand some of it. Madame Courbet hesitated before picking up the cross. Her hand hovered over the medal, as though she were afraid to touch it. When she did, she gently lifted it up and turned it over to read the inscription on the back. Then she pressed it to her breast and said, "Please come with me."

Twyla and her mother followed Madame Courbet to the back of the shop, through a curtained doorway to a sitting room in the rear. As they passed the kitchen, Madame Courbet told a young woman at work there to take charge of the shop for a while.

She asked Mrs. Jones and Twyla to be seated on an old settee. She sat opposite them in a straight-backed chair. The room was spotless and the smell of baking bread lingered in the air. It was a homey room, old-fashioned and crowded with furniture. There were doilies on the tables and on the backs and arms of chairs. Every surface was covered with knickknacks. The collection included a variety of German ceramic dolls and paperweights with tiny dried flowers suspended inside.

Dozens of family photographs decorated the mantelpiece and tables. Twyla recognized Madame Courbet in some of the pictures. A young woman who appeared in some of them must be Theresa, Twyla thought. She studied the face closely. If it was Theresa, then the two old Maquis agents had been correct about her beauty.

Madame Courbet had regained her rigid posture. Her face was set as though she expected bad news.

Mrs. Jones cleared her throat and said something in French. Then she turned to Twyla and said, "The first thing you must do is to apologize to Madame Courbet."

"But I could never say all that in French."

"I'll translate," her mother answered.

Twyla began, feeling her throat tighten and her face strain. "I am very sorry we frightened you in the church the other day," she said.

Mrs. Jones translated and Madame Courbet looked at Twyla with a puzzled expression. She didn't seem to know what Twyla was referring to.

Twyla continued, "Marie and I were in the church, looking at the relic on the altar. We were at the back, near the confession booth, when you came in. I'm not sure why we stayed there so long, but when you started to leave we were afraid you would think that we were spying on you, so we stayed hidden in the confessional."

Twyla stopped. Her mother repeated the explanation in French and she saw the glimmer of recognition appear in Madame Courbet's eyes. Before Twyla could finish the story Madame Courbet walked toward her, took a doily off the arm of the chair, and held it up to Twyla's face, covering all but her eyes.

Twyla's eyes were as wide with fright as they had been that day in church. Madame Courbet studied her face, then said, "Brynna!"

Twyla couldn't face her at that moment. Instead she looked down at her hands clasped together on her lap.

Madame Courbet removed the doily and sat down again. When Twyla looked up she was surprised to see that the woman was smiling. It was an odd smile, as though her facial muscles were not used to the exercise.

Twyla felt better now that the apology had been made, but she still had to relate the story about the search for Charles LaVesque.

"Start at the beginning," her mother urged gently.

Twyla spoke quickly. She wanted to end the visit with Madame Courbet as soon as possible. Her mother translated as Twyla spoke. Madame Courbet did not seem angry. In fact, she seemed glad to hear Twyla's tale, especially about the meeting with the two agents of the Maquis. She nodded with approval when Twyla spoke of visiting Theresa's grave.

"It was good of you to go there. I do not get there often enough," she murmured.

Finally Twyla reached one of the most critical parts of her story — that Charles LaVesque was not a fugitive. She explained that he no longer needed to hide, because he had been exonerated of any wrongdoing years before.

"Monsieur Dotti said a medal should be given to LaVesque for his bravery against the Nazis. If only we could find him," Twyla finished.

Madame Courbet's smile faded. She shook her head and said, "I hope it is not too late, but I fear the worst. I have not seen him since that day you were in the shop with Marie. He came to say good-by to me, also. I tried to persuade him to stay, but he would not. He never would stay with me. Several years ago he was in this part of France and visited the shop often, but he never told me where or how he lived. He wanted it that way. There was nothing I could do."

She held the cross reverently in her hands and asked, "May I keep this?"

When her mother had translated this, Twyla said, "Of course. You have more right to it than anyone else."

Madame Courbet said, "It really belongs to Charles. But I will keep it until he can be found."

Madame Courbet's comment about Charles brought the meeting to an end. Twyla had accomplished what she had come to do. But she still had not found Charles LaVesque. It was an unsolved part of the mystery that would haunt her forever, she thought.

She and her mother prepared to leave. Madame Courbet stood in the center of the sitting room with the cross in her hands and a warm smile on her face.

She said, "The legend of Brynna does not promise us what form the saint will take when she appears. I believe I did see her in the confessional, Twyla." She held up the Cross of Lorraine and added, in English this time, "Thank you."

16

The Tunnel

The rest of the weekend passed quietly at the bunker. Nicholas and Bernard spent all their time in the cavern skateboarding. Mrs. Jones and Madame Lambert were busy cooking and painting and reminiscing. Twyla read.

Once she followed the boys downstairs to see how well Bernard was learning to skateboard. Bernard made her feel so unwelcome that she soon returned to her room and book.

She slept well Saturday night. Her mother always said that there is no better sleeping potion than a clear conscience. It seemed to be true in Twyla's case. The meeting with Madame Courbet had cleared her mind of one troubling problem. But the mystery of Charles La-

Vesque's present whereabouts, or even whether he was alive, still remained. Madame Courbet had promised to let them know whenever he was found. Twyla realized that this could be months or even years, though the promise of some day knowing the outcome was comforting.

By Sunday Twyla was already looking forward to Monday morning, when Marie would return. Then they could explore the new tunnel entrance she had found.

On Sunday night Twyla was particularly restless. It was late when she finished reading a mystery book and dropped it into her suitcase. Awake and active since dawn, she should have been tired, but was not. She wandered upstairs to brew a cup of hot chocolate. Her mother and Madame Lambert were still up, sitting on the deck, enjoying the fine weather that had returned that afternoon.

Twyla joined them in the soft velvet night. The black sky was pierced with countless bright stars. All below was in darkness. The deck was illuminated by lamplight, turned low so as not to interfere with stargazing.

"Lovely, isn't it?" her mother said as Twyla joined them.

Twyla said it was and took a seat near the rail, sipping her hot chocolate slowly. How peaceful the world seemed. She hoped it could always remain peaceful, so there would be no need to erect more monuments like those she had seen near Verdun.

"Cécile and I are planning an excursion to Strasbourg tomorrow," Mrs. Jones said. "I want to get some crystal and Cécile knows just the place to buy it at a bargain. Would you and Marie like to join us?"

Twyla hesitated. There was just one thing she wanted to do tomorrow and it had nothing to do with her mother's proposal.

"You don't have to go if you don't want to," her mother added. "The boys have already told me they would prefer staying home."

Madame Lambert said, "I am so happy Bernard has found an interest outside his books and maps. And I think he is already looking more robust, don't you?"

Her companion agreed. "Yes. I'm happy to see him more active and ready for adventure."

Twyla was relieved that she could stay home if she wished. She and Marie would have to sneak away from the boys so they could explore the tunnel alone, but that would not be difficult. All Bernard and Nicholas wanted to do these days was skateboard.

"That's settled then," said Mrs. Jones. "We can get an early start so we will be back by midafternoon."

"Perhaps you and Marie can prepare lunch for Bernard and Nicky," Madame Lambert said.

"Oh, yes," said Twyla. "And I'll help Marie with her chores."

"Good," said Mrs. Jones. "Then you girls will have more time to visit with each other. I'm so happy you have Marie for company. I think she has taught you much about France and the French way of life."

Madame Lambert said, apologetically, "I am sorry Bernard was not as good a host as he might have been.

Still, there is not much to do out here in the country. When you visit us in Paris this winter he will show you the city. It should be fun for you."

Twyla said, "Yes," but secretly she was not so sure she wanted to be introduced to Paris by Bernard.

She was about to say good night and return to her room when she became aware of the same rhythmic thumping she had heard Friday night. It was the heartbeat of the hill again, barely audible. It was more of a feeling than a sound. The wooden deck seemed to vibrate with it.

"What is that curious vibration?" Twyla's mother asked. "I'm sure I felt it last night."

They listened for a few moments; then Madame Lambert said, "This old place is so full of sounds, one never can tell."

Twyla said, "It seems to come from the walls. Thump, thump, thump."

Madame Lambert shrugged. "It could be the pipes. We had many strange plumbing noises when we first put in our modern pipes. The plumber theorized that air was trapped in the pipes."

Twyla did not think it sounded like trapped air. "It seems to be farther away than that," she said.

"Perhaps it comes from the old system of vents and air conditioners that are buried throughout the hill," Madame Lambert suggested. "Water from the recent rains could be dripping somewhere. Or it could be animals — "

"I know," said Mrs. Jones. "You needn't remind me

of the little furry creatures crawling through the old tunnels."

The women laughed. When they stopped they noticed the sound had stopped, too.

Mrs. Jones said, "Maybe it's a ghost. I would prefer a ghost to a rat in the tunnel."

Twyla returned to her room aware that she did not share her mother's sentiments. She would rather have a rat for a tunnel companion. She'd had enough of ghosts.

The fresh air and hot chocolate had made her drowsy. She was soon asleep. She woke up once thinking she heard the thumping noise again, but the sound stopped by the time she was fully awake. She fell asleep once more and slept until morning without any interruptions.

Her mother and Madame Lambert were ready to leave for Strasbourg when Twyla came to the breakfast table. The boys had eaten and stayed just long enough to say good-by to their mothers, then vanished in the direction of the underground skating room.

Soon Marie joined Twyla at the breakfast table, where Twyla told her of the dramatic visit to Madame Courbet's bakery and home. A short time later the girls were ready for the exploration. They started up the road to the secret entrance.

"I promised Madame Lambert that we would prepare lunch for Bernard and Nicholas," Twyla told Marie. "That gives us over two hours to explore the tunnel."

Marie wore tennis shoes and jeans like Twyla, so she would be comfortable hiking. Still, she didn't seem as eager as Twyla about the tunnel expedition.

"Won't it be too dark to see in the tunnel?" she asked.

Twyla patted her hip pocket and said, "That's why I brought the flashlight."

"Perhaps it is unsafe. You said the other tower was in ruins."

"Don't worry," said Twyla. "If we run into any place that seems unsafe we will turn back."

"Still . . ." Marie began.

"Stop worrying. As far as I explored in the tunnel, it seemed solid and undamaged." Twyla stopped on the road opposite the logs she had used as a landmark. She faced Marie and asked, "Aren't you curious to see what may be built into this part of the hill?"

Marie was not curious, but she followed as Twyla led the way off the road, through the ditch, and into the thick growth of trees. Marie showed more interest when Twyla stopped in front of the vines that shrouded the hillside.

Twyla lifted the loose hanging vines and with mock politeness said, "After you, *mademoiselle.*"

Marie stepped through the opening and into the mouth of the tunnel. Twyla followed, first making sure that the vines swung back into place. They stood for a few minutes in silence absorbing the atmosphere of the quiet, secret place.

Finally Marie said, "It is not as spooky as I thought it might be. In fact it is rather nice — peaceful and private."

Twyla saw her friend glance with misgivings up into the dark tunnel beyond the entrance. She laughed and said, "Keep talking like that and you will have no trouble. I'm a little frightened myself, truthfully. But there is nothing here to be afraid of, unless you are afraid of rabbits, mice, and bats."

"Are there bats?" Marie asked.

"I didn't see any before. But if bats live in the tunnel they shouldn't bother us. They are nocturnal."

She took the flashlight out of her pocket and led the way up the tunnel. The meager light from the veiled tunnel entrance soon faded and they had to rely entirely on the flashlight.

"Watch out for the groove in the middle of the floor," Twyla warned.

Marie, walking safely a step behind Twyla, saw the hazard. Their footfalls echoed eerily, the sound mingling with occasional rustlings that could have been made by mice or rabbits.

Twyla felt a tug on her shirt, where Marie held on for moral, if not physical, support. Soon they came to an opening on the right-hand side of the tunnel. Twyla turned her light in that direction and they saw a large cavern similar to the one that Bernard and Nicholas used for skateboarding. This one, however, had not been swept clean, like the Lamberts' future mushroom room. There were cobwebs hanging from the lichen-covered ceiling and the floor was littered with straw. They were startled by a pair of beady eyes staring at them from a pile of wooden crates heaped up in one corner. The air in the room smelled of mold, rotted wood, and another odor that Twyla didn't care to identify.

"Like death," Marie whispered in her ear, as though she had read Twyla's thoughts.

From the cavern they stepped back into the tunnel, where the air seemed fresh by comparison.

"Shall we go back now?" Marie asked.

"We've just begun," Twyla responded. "We have nothing to fear. Look at the walls and ceilings. They are strong and sound."

She flashed the light around so Marie could see the solid cement that surrounded them. Cobwebs and fungus gave the only hint of age.

The tunnel ended abruptly where it intersected another passageway. Littering the intersection were piles of paper, old cartons, rotted wooden crates, and a stack of lumber. The girls picked their way through the mess carefully, then stopped while Twyla again moved the beam of light in all directions.

To the left this new tunnel seemed to turn a corner about fifty feet away. To the right the tunnel led into a room at the far reaches of her light.

"Which way?" Twyla asked.

"Does it matter?" Marie wailed.

Twyla thought a moment, then said, "The left must lead toward the Lamberts' bunker. We can explore there later. Let's go this way."

She and Marie started moving to the right. At that moment they heard a strange noise. A chain clanked with a ringing sound. This was followed by muffled footsteps that seemed to come from all around them. Marie let go of Twyla's shirt and both girls stood still.

"Someone's coming!" said Twyla.

"What shall we do?" Marie cried.

"This way," said Twyla, hastening toward the entrance to the room at the end of the tunnel.

As she ran the sounds around her grew louder. The sounds were followed by an ominous rhythmic thumping noise that was deafening. Twyla reached the end of the tunnel and was about to duck through the doorway when she slipped and began to fall.

She reached out for support but found none. She landed hard on her stomach on the cold floor as the flashlight flew from her hands.

She must have blacked out for a moment, because she had no memory of anything except the deafening sound when she fell. As her senses returned, she began coughing from the thick cloud of dust that had risen all around her. Her fright grew when she discovered that she could not move her left leg.

She choked as she gulped for air.

"Marie!" she cried. "Marie, are you all right?"

Twyla's own weak voice bounced back and then the air was still. A few feet ahead of her lay the flashlight, still shining. Its beam barely lit up the room in which she now lay. It seemed smaller than the cavern they had passed on their way, and it was filled with chunks of cement and loose earth. Buried beneath the debris were pieces of furniture, including a cot and a table. Broken pieces of crockery lay on the floor near her head.

Twyla tried to turn over onto her back but found it impossible. Her left foot was pinned down by the debris.

For the first time she realized what had happened. There had been a cave-in!

It seemed a long time before Twyla heard voices from the other side of the fallen debris. But actually it was just a few minutes later. The first voice she heard was Marie's, calling her name. Then she heard other voices join Marie's. They were shouting now and she recognized Nicholas's voice and then heard Bernard saying, "If she is under that pile then we're too late."

That shows how much he knows, Twyla thought.

"I'm here!" she called back. "Under the rocks."

She heard Marie squeal. Then Twyla saw a finger of light coming through the wall of debris above her foot.

"Can you see her?" Nicholas cried.

"No," Bernard answered. Then he called, "Are you completely buried, Twyla?"

"No, of course not," she answered, feeling herself grow impatient as her fear subsided. "Only one foot is pinned down."

"Can you move it at all?" Bernard asked her from the other side of the wall of cement blocks.

Twyla moved her left foot from side to side. "I can move it a little," she answered. "But it hurts."

She worked her foot back and forth gently, at the same time pulling it toward her. Then, by a stroke of good luck, Twyla's leg slipped out from beneath the rock and she rolled over on her back, with a feeling of great relief.

"I'm free!" she yelled. "I'm O.K."

She heard a chorus of cheers answer her words. Then Bernard said, "Good. Now just stay where you are while I see if we can move these blocks and get you out safely. Don't touch anything!"

His last order irked her. Why was it that Bernard always brought out that response in her, even when he was trying to help? She had to admit, however, that his advice was good, so she sat still. Bernard was deciding what to do next.

She could hear the buzz of their voices as they discussed the problem. Then Bernard announced, "Marie is going for help. Nicholas and Gitano will stay here and keep you company, and I am going to my bunker to get some tools. Will you be all right for a while?"

"Yes, I'm all right," she said, rubbing her aching ankle.

"It may be a while, Twyla," he continued. "Marie will have to go to the road and flag down someone to go for help. Don't be afraid. We'll have you out soon."

"I'm not afraid," she said, and wished it were true. She was beginning to realize the seriousness of her position.

When Marie and Bernard had gone Nicholas's small voice asked, "How did you get in the tunnel?"

"I found another entrance down by the road," she answered. "But how did you and Bernard get here?"

"That was our secret," Nicholas answered. "We've been working on that wall down in the skating room. We just finished today and started exploring. I was going to tell you, Twyla, but Bernard said it would be our surprise. We were going to tell you after we got the wall opened up today, but we couldn't find you and Marie, so we came alone."

Twyla was glad they had come. Otherwise she and Marie could have been trapped for a long time. In a flash of insight she realized that she was the only one who had been trapped by the cave-in.

"Nicholas, what happened to Marie? Why wasn't she caught by the falling cement, as I was?"

"Marie said she became confused. When the noise started, she ran the other way. Boy, she sure scared us! We thought she was a ghost. I thought Bernard would break through a wall when he saw her coming straight at us out of the black tunnel."

Twyla heard Nicholas chuckle and she smiled herself as she imagined the scene.

"You guys sure were noisy," she said.

"Were we? If we were loud, you and Marie sounded like you were knocking down the whole bunker!"

Twyla started to say, "You mean that wasn't you making the noise I heard before the cave-in?" then stopped.

The thumping noise had begun again, filling the room with a deafening roar. Suddenly it stopped and Twyla heard from behind her in the same room a real live ghostlike groan.

17

Twyla Meets a Ghost

The echoes of the groan stopped and the underground room was quiet again.

"Wh-what was that?" Nicholas asked from the other side of the heap of broken boards and cement.

"I'm not sure, Nicky. But don't run away," Twyla said.

Her brother's voice came back full of false bravado. "I wouldn't do that. I wouldn't leave you alone. Besides, we have Gitano here to protect us."

Twyla heard the dog's collar clink and Gitano's whine. She could picture her brother hanging on to him tightly. She wished the dog were on her side of the stone pile, to give her the moral support she needed.

"I'm O.K., Nicky, but I must find out what's happening in this room. Don't move."

She picked up her flashlight. The light was growing dim and she hoped the batteries would last until she was rescued. She moved cautiously around the room. A huge mound of blocks and dirt was piled at one end. Above the mound she could see a wide hole. The flashlight beam wasn't strong enough to reach far, but she could detect the remnants of a circular staircase. Twyla guessed that the staircase led to the dynamited tower at the top of the hill.

She climbed to the top of the mound and peered over to the other side. A scrap of cloth poking out of the debris attracted her. She crept closer to inspect it and recognized the tarpaulinlike material. Twyla had seen it twice before, once on the road to the bunker and once in St. Germain. Both times it had been worn by the man she now knew was Charles LaVesque.

The pieces of the puzzle all fit together. She was in LaVesque's hideaway. That's why he left their car, so close to the Lamberts' bunker, the night of their arrival. He probably had a secret path leading through the woods directly to the entrance under the vines.

She walked to the other side of the rubble and there, lying immobile on his back, was Charles LaVesque! He lay clear of the rubble, close to an old exposed water pipe that had been torn from its place near the ceiling. LaVesque's arm was stretched out on the floor next to the pipe. In his fist he clenched a long bar of iron.

He lay still. Twyla flashed her light on his face. His eyes were closed and the skin under a stubbly growth of beard was a lifeless gray. Twyla's first impression was that LaVesque had been killed by the cave-in. Then she was amazed to see the arm holding the iron bar slowly rise in the air and bang the water pipe.

Suddenly, the underground room was filled again with the familiar sound of rhythmic thumps as Charles La-Vesque, more dead than alive, beat out the signal for help that he had been beating for the last few days.

Twyla realized that there must have been an earlier cave-in, maybe a few days ago, when he had become injured. And, unable to move, he had been signaling for help by banging on the water pipe.

She bent over him and put her hand on his forehead. "It's all right, Mr. LaVesque," she said, leaning close to his face. "You have been found. We'll have you out of here in a few minutes. Just be still and . . . and . . ."

There were no more words to say. She continued to pat his forehead, which felt cold and damp. She was not sure that he was conscious enough to hear her, but his arm fell back to the floor and his hand opened, releasing the tire iron.

Twyla went to the cot, tore off two old army blankets, and hurried back to cover him. She found a pillow half buried in the dirt and placed it under his head. Then she went to the pile of debris that blocked the doorway and called to Nicholas.

"I'm still here," he answered. "What's going on, anyway?"

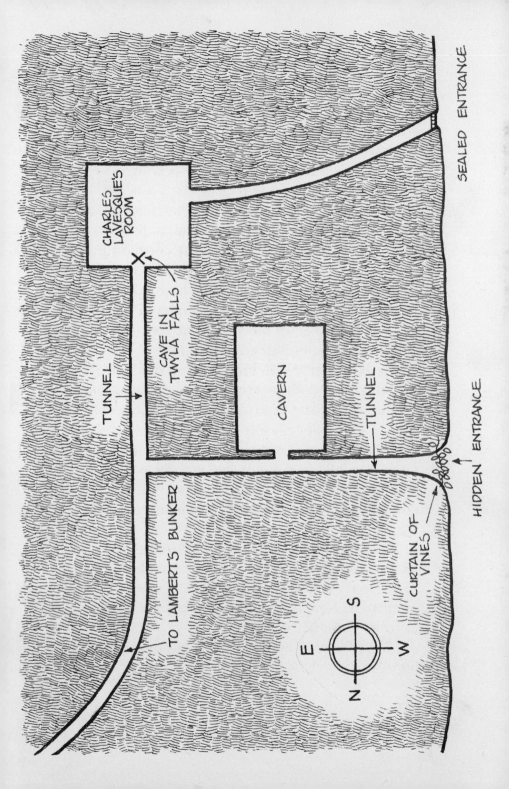

"I've found Charles LaVesque," Twyla said. "He's still alive, but in very poor condition."

"Who is he? Twyla, what are you talking about?" Nicholas asked, his voice trembling.

Twyla had forgotten that Nicholas didn't know anything about Charles LaVesque. There was no time to explain now.

"It's the stranger whose bicycle we crashed into in the rain," she answered. "The man whose Cross of Lorraine you found. Now listen to me carefully."

Nicholas listened and repeated her orders. He was to find Bernard and explain about LaVesque, that the man had been injured and an ambulance should be called. Nicholas finally left in search of Bernard, but only after Twyla had pleaded with him, assuring him that she was safe and unhurt. Nicholas sputtered before running off that he had promised Bernard he would not leave her alone.

When he had gone, Twyla went back to Charles LaVesque and sat by him, holding his hands. By her friendly gestures she hoped to reassure him that he was no longer trapped alone in the bunker.

About a half-hour passed before Bernard and Nicholas returned. Twyla left LaVesque's side and went to the pile of rocks at the doorway.

"You still all right, Twyla?" Bernard called to her.

"Yes. Did you get help?"

"We flagged down a motorist on the road and told him about the injured man. Marie was gone, so she must have already gotten a ride to town. Help should arrive very soon. How is he?"

"He's still alive, but he is unconscious. Except for a bump on the head he doesn't seem to have any other injuries. I don't think any rocks or debris fell on him. I think his head hit a rock when he fell down and he was knocked unconscious."

"How heavy is the damage in there?" Bernard asked.

"It looks like the whole top of the bunker fell in. I'm sure there has been more than one cave-in. I think this room is right under the dynamited tower on top."

"I thought the same. Can you see anything?"

Twyla described the room, telling Bernard that further cave-ins were possible. Bernard was alarmed by her report. "Stay away from the opening," he said.

"But Charles LaVesque is lying right under more rocks and concrete that may fall."

"We can't do anything about that now, Twyla. You stay clear. No sense in your being killed too if more debris falls. Find a good solid section of ceiling to sit under. Better than that, if you can find a strong table lie under it."

Twyla did as she was told. It felt good to have someone take charge and tell her what to do. And Bernard definitely had taken charge. He sounded much older now as he gave orders to Nicholas on the other side of the rubble.

"What are you doing?" Twyla asked.

"I found some wood back in the tunnel. I want to try to shore up the ceiling on this side so no more cement will fall on us," Bernard answered. "Then we can start removing some of the rocks in the doorway."

Twyla listened as they worked. Periodically she crawled over the pile of debris to check on Charles La-Vesque. His condition hadn't changed. She could feel his pulse, though it was weak. His breathing was regular but shallow. It seemed to her that his face was more peaceful than when she had first found him. Although still unconscious, he may have become aware that he had been found and rescue was near. She hoped so.

From her safe position under the table, Twyla inspected the remains of the room. LaVesque's bicycle was lying behind the cot. She recognized it as the same battered vehicle he had ridden in the rain and again in St. Germain. Nearby were tools and a workbench. One slab of cement had partially buried the bench and scattered his tools over the floor. LaVesque had set up an extensive work area before the cave-in. Now Twyla was sure that on her first night in the bunker it was LaVesque repairing his bicycle that she had heard.

She made another discovery that would please Nicholas. There was his model dirigible, lying on the floor near the workbench. She wondered whether Charles LaVesque had found it and brought it to his work area to repair before returning it to Nicholas.

Twyla might never know the answer, but the fact that the dirigible was here was proof that Charles LaVesque had been up and around the day they flew the dirigible on the hilltop.

Twyla heard a commotion in the tunnel: help had

finally arrived from the village. She moved closer to the blocked doorway to listen. She heard excited voices speaking in French, and footsteps approaching.

At one point she could faintly detect a conversation between a man and Bernard. The man seemed to be praising Bernard for the work he had done shoring up the ceiling. She heard the rescue team go to work removing blocks of cement and fallen dirt. Finally, enough of the obstacles had been removed so that she could see through to the other side.

The first person she saw on the other side was Nicholas, looking anxious and adorable. She could have hugged him, so great was her love for him at that moment. Instead, she handed him his dirigible and said, "Look what I found."

"Golly!" was his response.

Bernard reached in to help her through the opening. He led her to a stretcher and insisted she lie down on it.

"You have to, Twyla," he said, concern and admiration showing in his eyes. "The ambulance attendants say you must — just in case any bones are broken."

After he made sure she was comfortable, he returned to the cave-in to aid in the rescue of Charles LaVesque. Twyla was whisked down through the tunnel to an ambulance parked on the road below. There was another ambulance waiting for LaVesque.

As they drove by the Lamberts' bunker Twyla saw Madame Lambert's car turning into the road.

"Stop!" Twyla shouted to the driver and his attendant. "There's my mother."

The ambulance stopped. Twyla's mother and Madame Lambert were beside it in seconds. The ambulance driver told them about the successful rescue mission. Her mother stepped into the vehicle beside Twyla and rode with her to the clinic in the village. On the short drive to St. Germain Twyla told her mother all that had happened that day.

Later that evening a convivial group gathered around the fireplace in the Lamberts' bunker home. Mrs. Jones and Madame Lambert had prepared a buffet supper for the group, which included Marie and her uncle Monsieur Duran, who had led the rescue party from the village. Madame Courbet was there, too. She sat upright on the sofa next to Twyla, in her prim black dress. She seemed to be happy and relieved. Around her neck was her sister's Cross of Lorraine.

"I will give it back to Charles as soon as he is conscious enough to recognize me," she had told them.

Twyla's ankle was taped and propped up on a cushion, the only evidence in the room of the near tragedy that had occurred that day. The same doctor in the clinic at St. Germain had treated both Twyla and Charles LaVesque. He had assured them that LaVesque would be awake and starting to recover by morning; he had suffered a head concussion but seemed to be in good health otherwise.

"I cannot understand why he thought he was dying," Madame Courbet told them. "I think he was just suffering from tiredness brought on by age and by his unending loneliness. But he will be alone no longer. I shall insist he move to my home when he leaves the clinic. I can care for him in his old age and he need not ever again roam the country like a homeless refugee."

"How long do you think he lay there before you found him today?" Mrs. Jones asked her daughter.

Twyla hesitated briefly and then answered, "I've been trying to figure that out. The first time I heard the thumping noise was the night we returned from Verdun. That was Friday."

"Three days ago!" Madame Lambert exclaimed. "It is a wonder he survived so long."

"I did hear a softer tapping noise on our first night here," Twyla said. "But it was a different kind of sound and I think I know now what that was. I think the tapping was done by Monsieur LaVesque while repairing his bicycle after it had been hit by our car."

Her mother nodded. "He must have gone to that room right after we let him out on the road."

"There were other mysterious noises, too," Twyla said. Bernard looked her way and they stared at each other for a moment before she went on. "But they came from this end of the bunker," she said without elaborating. "It was the smell of garlic that really should have signaled us that someone was living down there. Monsieur LaVesque evidently loves garlic in his cooking."

Madame Courbet agreed when Twyla's words were translated for her. She told them that the aroma of garlic surrounded LaVesque whenever he came to visit her. She added with a smile that he would have to be content

175

with a little less garlic in his food when he came to live with her.

Monsieur Duran spoke up then. "I inspected the room that collapsed. It is a wonder it didn't cave in years ago. It had been weakened when the tower above was destroyed right after the war. Charles LaVesque was living under a time bomb."

Twyla sat back with a contented smile beaming at everyone. It was such a good feeling to have all the mysteries solved.

"It's been a busy week," she sighed.

Her mother laughed. "You now have another week to relax and enjoy your stay in France, and to recuperate before we leave to join Father in Frankfurt," she said.

Twyla was eager to tell her father all about her adventure in France. He often told her that her curiosity would get her into trouble someday. But this time it had led to the rescue of Charles LaVesque, and she knew he would be proud.

Still, the thought of leaving the Lamberts saddened her. The adventures of the day in the tunnel had brought out a side of Bernard she hadn't suspected. He was capable of decisive action in an emergency. Also, he made no effort to hide his concern about her well-being since her rescue. He even told her how much he admired the brave way she had acted while trapped behind the wall of rubble. Her opinion of Bernard was changing with each comment. She now looked forward to seeing him in Paris. And perhaps next summer they could again visit the Lamberts in the bunker.

"In spite of all the danger and risk, I have enjoyed this week," Twyla said with enthusiasm.

Her mother looked at her sternly and said, "I know you have. But for the rest of our time here you must promise not to go off exploring in the tunnels."

"I promise," she said, reluctantly.

"I have other plans for this week," Bernard offered. "I still have not mastered the skateboard."

"And all this time I thought that was what you and Nicky were doing down below," Twyla said.

Bernard grinned. "I only had one lesson. That was the one you gave me the first night you went exploring."

Twyla returned his smile, remembering his awkwardness on the board. "Then it's safe to say that we will be very busy indeed this week," she said.

They all laughed.

Madame Courbet had a puzzled look on her face as she asked, "*Qu'est-ce que c'est que ce* skateboard?"

As the fire flickered, turning to embers, and the stars came out, the children tried to explain to a bewildered Madame Courbet the art of the American sport of skateboarding.

Nicholas got his board out to demonstrate his skill on the hearth. Twyla knew she would remember forever the scene of Madame Courbet sitting near the fire trying to figure out how to "hang ten."